The Glistening
A Group Project
Aria Daze

Daze Dream Publications

Contents

Also by Aria Daze

Dedicated to greedy bisexuals.
You can have it all and in fact, you deserve it. Never change, darlings.

Content Warnings!

PLEASE READ!

B efore you dive in, please check out these handy content warnings. Reading should be enjoyable, and some of the topics covered in this book may not be for you. Your mental health matters.

This book will include the following:

- Alcohol consumption
- Death of a parent (Mentioned briefly)
- Petty theft
- Witch craft
- Men exchanging fisticuffs
- Gang bangs
- Oral sex
- Homosexual activity of multiple varieties
- Pooh Kink
- Group Sex
- Foul language

This book also features black people who utilize Ebonics in their speech. It's not country, improper, or ghetto, and I would not like to see any emails about it. Please feel free to email me about other things though, such as the honey scene. As always, if any of these topics sound unpleasant to you, please do not continue onward, dear reader. I have other books in my catalog that may be a better fit such as Rudy Jones's New Year's Resolution. The Glistening is also an erotica, so please expect it to be about 60% sex. **This book is not suitable for readers under the age of 18!**

THE PLAYLIST

- LULLABY-A'MAAL NUUX FT. SYD
- VIBES-SEBASTIAN MIKAEL
- CHERRY BLOSSOMS- KYLE DION
- WHEN WE-TANK
- GHOST RIDE- BLK ODDSSEY
- ORANGE WINE- BLK ODDSSEY
- BAD DREAM/NO LOOKING BACK-SYD
- TOUCH ME-VICTORIA MONET
- VIXEN-MIGUEL

Chapter 1

Genesis

M aia

It was the 21st morning of September, and I mourned the end of vacation season with the hand-warming comfort of a cinnamon-heavy champurrado. Summertime was over and Autumn was in full swing. Sunset-colored trees were losing leaves like strippers were losing panties, the morning air was always chilly and dripping with dew, and the sunsets were always crisp and breezy. Halloween decorations were being thrown up everywhere, and the year end festivities were kicking up, which is why I shouldn't have been surprised when I received *it*.

The invitation that was poking out of my mailbox like a thorn.

I looked at the gold-embossed card and then channeled my inner poltergeist with an obnoxious groan. Samara's Halloween parties were legendary, but I hadn't been to one since me and, *The One Who Shall Not Be Named*, broke up. The memory of that night was bad enough, but the invitation also taunted me with a courteous option for a non-existent plus one. This was my second Halloween single and even the paper ghost displays on my neighbors windows were starting to irritate me. Mostly because they were all booed up. Literally. Everyone was booed up it seemed. All my friends were thriving on the West Coast in their happy little relationships. Everywhere I looked I saw people planning couples costumes, and there were already Christmas sweetheart ads playing. Yet, here I was.

With my only guest of honor being a well-ridden Sybian.

Don't get me wrong, the single life had its perks. Hoeing being one of them. I loved sampling from the single platter. However, when our Group Trip came around and everyone was headed home, heads resting on their partner's shoulders in the busy departure terminal, cozy, comfortable, and well-fucked, a jolt of longing shot through me. I wanted that and I used to have it before that nigga ruined everything. Sure, I theoretically could've forgiven him, but the thought of easing my boundaries for a *man* made me want to jump in the Chattahoochee and let a snapping turla eat my coochie.

The admittedly ugly ring didn't bother me, nor did his strange obsession with tighty-whities, or his receding hairline.
I could look past plenty of things, but cheating, especially while in a polyamorous relationship was not one of them. Who the fuck does that anyway? Imagine being given keys to a full garage then still choosing to steal a bicycle. That's what finding out felt like. Especially when I had to explain why I was calling off our wedding after ten years! I cried to my Granny for forty days and forty nights. I never planned to be on the dating scene again but suddenly I was thrust into it like a nervous understudy. I was always happy with him and my friends. The problem was that I assumed he was too.

That's why older folks say to assume is to make an ass out of you and me. I assumed he was happy, and just like a man, he chose to embarrass me. But I couldn't let him take all the blame for the embarrassment part. The way I had initially reacted when I found out was a bit less than mature, especially considering we were at Sam's Halloween party when it happened. Sucking his cousin's dick on the band stage to get back at him wasn't my finest moment, but damn was it fun. Especially since Kaylin's was bigger. Now that I thought about it, taking the girl he cheated on me with home probably wasn't all that great of a choice either. Still, I didn't have regrets, especially since her pussy was fire and she reminded me that I could cash in my mattress warranty and get rid of any trace of that nigga.

Plus all of that bullshit kicked off my secondary hoe phase. It was my firmest belief that every woman should have a hoe phase. I had a starter one in college when I first met Daya and Dolly. While it was cute and all it didn't have shit on my grown-woman sexpedition. I had a revolving door of weekly flavors, night caps, and daily breads. Who had time to grieve a broken heart when they were getting head on a mechanical bull? I was hunching so much that I could see the judgement visible in my gyno's eyes when I went to get my weekly test, and if the sex hadn't been so damn good I might have even gave a fuck. Luckily, and unfortunately, that dynasty didn't last long. I had friends who loved me, and I was used to being valued. That wasn't a guarantee with casual sex. So I quickly got over the novelty of unattachment. After seeing the plus one option on the invitation, I was starting to crave something different.

Something real.
I wanted to date again.

Lucianna

"Ugh, I want a girlfriend," I pouted, throwing down my phone. My FYPs were full of thick dark skin women shaking ass, and even though I was guilty of the occasional saved video, I still had no idea why it was so persistent. Maybe it was a sign from the universe.
"You know, you say that every week. I think I'd be offended if you weren't face down, ass up snoring, every other night."
I untucked myself from the massive quilt draped across the bed before rolling over to face Erm. His brows were tight, attempting to convey something akin to austerity, only for him to erupt into belly-shaking laughter seconds later.
"Ermias," I pouted again. "That's not funny. You're supposed to be helping me with this."
"Ok, baby. I'm sorry," he conceded with one last chuckle. "Who's your ideal woman?"
"Honestly? Nicole Byer."
Erm burst into another fit of echoing laughter. This time I knew why. Unfortunately I was born too Black and too female to be Nicole's type, but a girl could dream. Right?

"Luci, I'm a wingman not a magician," he snickered, forcing me to consider an actual answer.
"I don't know," I groaned. "Ideally a girl's girl. Someone I can wake up early with for farmer's markets, estate sales, and breakfast. Somebody who wants to get matching nails with me. You know I like coordinating."
"Mhm, you sure do," he nodded.
"Also big titties are a plus," I added.
"That's superficial, Luc."
"Ok fine, let's hear about your dream girl then!" I scoffed while lighting an incense.
If we were going to talk about it, I might as well go to work manifesting it. My motto had increasingly become, good things come to those who take action.

"Well, I'm talking to mine," he cooed, pecking my forehead.
My damn heart skipped all over the place.
I had plenty of reasons why I loved autumn, but seeing Ermias' eyes twinkle against the warm candle light on a chilly evening was by far my favorite one. A lot of people claimed that marriage is where romance and effort went to die, but I never had that problem. It had been five years since we said I Do, and I still had a vase full of fresh flowers every Thursday, purses that were purely ornamental when we went out together, and

a standing Saturday night date that always ended in cuddles. Ermias had hearts in his eyes practically every time we talked. Which is why I never minded sharing his love. He had plenty to go around.

"I know I'm perfect and all, but I'm curious what our missing piece looks like to you," I whispered while snuggling against his chest.

"Tall, because my back hurts from bending all the time," he yawned in between hushed laughter.

He preemptively flinched because while I wasn't jealous of much, I resented my short stature. I was only 5'4 and I hated it. I couldn't even reach the good plates on the top shelf of the pantry without help.

"Chile anyways," I tutted. "Anything else?"

"I'm just fucking with you Luci, but I don't know. Maybe somebody who's interested in horticulture. You don't care about plants unless they're actively flowering. Oh, and some-body who'll go to the range with me. I also wouldn't mind a fellow scotch enthusiasts, and also your words, not mine, somebody with big titties."

My molasses eyes met his hazel ones silently, then we held each other's tight gaze until I finally cracked and burst into laughter.

"Whew, what a list," I chuckled. "We'd be better off trying to start a new religion."

"Hey, come on. Don't be like that," Erm chided. "We gotta speak stuff into existence no matter how delusional it sounds. Our dream lady is out there."

"Yes," I agreed with a nod. "Probably out there in Antarctica knowing our luck."

I extinguished the flame of the incense and then felt the tingle of magic race across my skin. I didn't recite a spell, at least not on purpose. Yet there was strange energy lingering in the air.

"Maybe, but maybe not," Ermias grinned.

Chapter 2

Falling

Maia

Somehow we were at the end of October and we still had days that were a thousand damn degrees. I missed Florida at times because at least the marshes kept it cool at night. The sun went down 2 hours ago and Decatur was still humid as fuck. Not even Trader Joe's industrial air conditioning could fight it.

"I thought you had one of them?" Granny asked, poking around in my basket.

She was referring to my new monstera, and while I technically had *two* of them at home, neither was a Thai Constellation.

"Bert and Ernie are lonely, they need a friend," I shrugged.

"Is this yo way of telling me you're in a three-way?" Granny queried while side-eyeing my plant.

"What no, lady! This is just my money-sucking habit. Some people buy crack, I buy plants."

"Don't get all fussy with me," she tutted. "It's a valid question. I still don't believe that you never dated your one brown skinned friend with the big booty. What's her name again?"

"Daya."

"Mhm, exactly," Granny nodded with a slick grin. "I know y'all kissed."

I would rather die by a thousand wasp stings than tell my 80 year old Geechee grandmother about my sex life, but she wasn't wrong. Me and Daya did kiss.

Everywhere.

Repeatedly.

"Daya is about to be happily engaged in LA, and I'm single as a Pringle in Atlanta, Granny Girl," I explained. "We do not go together."

"I said dated as in past tense, but alright My Mai. I'm ready for checkout."

Granny calling me My Mai made my heart squeeze even though she rode my nerves with all her questions. I swear she was a gossip reporter in her early days. She was getting her scoop by any means necessary. I wasn't her only victim either. Especially not tonight. I could see the chaos simmering in her eyes as she guided her buggy towards her favorite clerk's register.

Fifteen minutes and 3 coupons later, we were loading everything into the car. I invested in a truck for Saturday morning rummage sale finds, but it came in handy for other things. Things like my grandmother's random impulse buys.
"Granny, what are you gonna do with a half-pallet of frozen orange juice concentrate?" I sighed while hoisting the load into the bed.
"Our book club be making mimosas out of those," she explained. "It was a good deal. Plus I figured you could use some."

Of course she did. We both knew my love of orange juice was a problem. Financially, physically, hell, even spiritually. My version of Hell was a carton of the good stuff with only a swallow left in it for all eternity. Coincidentally, that was likely the most reasonable explanation for Granny's purchase.
"Stop trying to buy me stuff."
"No. You're my baby," she said with an unyielding scowl.

Technically she wasn't wrong. My parents were both enlisted when I was born, and in the interest of my stability, they gave me to my grandmother once I got big enough to talk. She didn't mind one bit from what she recalled, my momma was an only child, and for granny, raising me fulfilled the yearning she once had to have more. Unfortunately her raising me came after both my parents lost their lives over in Iraq.

The ride home was mostly quiet except for the occasional holler from somebody driving past us, the hum of the engine, the snap of fallen leaves, and the rattle of a year's worth of oj in the bed. It was the perfect autumn night. Right until we pulled into Granny's driveway.
"My Mai," she whispered cautiously as she reached across the console to pat my hand. "I think you should move to Los Angeles."

A quick chuckle escaped me before I realized that Granny was serious. Her eyes were solemn and shiny with unshed tears while her lips were pressed into a hard line. I hadn't seen her look that serious in well, ever. The proper thing to do would've been to console her or ask clarifying questions but I was ready to go home and ravage the container of hummus

I just bought. So instead, I took a deep, belly-bloating breath and burst out laughing.

"Claudette, don't stress me out. I'm not moving to LA," I chuckled dryly.

"Girl, I don't know who you think you calling Claudette, but Claudette fights unlike Granny."

Then she crossed her arms over her chest, daring me to try her. Fortunately I knew better. She might have been 80 years old and 150 pounds soaking wet, but I've witnessed both Claudette and Granny drag a bitch.

"Granny," I sighed.

"You're lonely, Maia. And don't sit up here and lie like you ain't. It's been two years since you dumped that bum. You deserve somebody to come home to, baby"

"Why do I need to move to find that?"

"Because if you don't you'll spend all your time fussing after me! You're my granddaughter, not no damn CNA!"

So that's what this was about?

See, four years ago I moved back home. I was teaching a class when I'd gotten a call from St. Bart's Memorial that a Miss Claudette Tinsley had been admitted due to a fall and would need emergency surgery. Of course I packed up my shit and caught the next flight out. But what was originally supposed to be staying for recovery and going back home to Florida turned into a permanent relocation. Granny had chronic mobility issues, even if she liked to pretend like she didn't, so I helped her with a few things. Errands, groceries, cleaning, sometimes when she had a particularly good tough week, cooking.

And Granny hated every second of it.

"Granny, I volunteered to come back home because I love you. Ain't nobody holding me hostage."

She frowned in reply. It wasn't because she didn't enjoy having me around, but because of the shifting dynamic. After spending her golden years getting me to adulthood, she acted like she was burdening me.

"Can I just remind you that you took care of me from 18 months all the way up to 18 years?" I sighed.

"No. That's what grownups are supposed to do. What, was I just supposed to abandon you and say good luck?"

"Do you not see the irony here?" I asked while pinching my brows together.

"Maia," she groaned. "That's different! You ain't have anybody else. I could hire a nurse."

"Granny, you tried that. You hated people digging around in your house and you cussed two out for talking to you crazy. Honestly, what is this about bec-"

"Maia," Granny said sternly. "You need to go find a man!"

I jumped up, hit my head on the roof, and then my mouth fell open in shock. Usually I had a decent poker face, but not tonight. Tonight, my eyebrows squeezed together like a nutsack that was about to bust, in sheer disbelief of her audacity.

"Or a woman, a them-them," she continued, after successfully stunning me into silence. "I don't care. I'm just tired of seeing you in the house unless I call or you're on vacation."

"This conversation has gotten out of hand," I groaned while clamping the bridge of my nose.

"Why, cause I'm right?" she harrumphed.

I started to argue but I came up short as I searched through my memories for contrary evidence. The last time I did anything outside was when Velma was in town, three months ago. Otherwise I went to work, grabbed a coffee occasionally, and sometimes fucked something on the weekends, but I hadn't done that in a minute. I was a shut in. I couldn't recall the last time I did anything with this ass other than sit on it. Could I even remember how to throw it back?

"Women are more than relationships. Isn't that what you told me?" I finally said, hoping to pry her off the topic.

"You want me to leave it alone, fine I will. But you can only buy so many batteries before it becomes a government concern," Granny tutted.

"They make rechargeable ones now," I grumbled while un-buckling my seat belt.

Usually I'd come in and sit a while, shoot the shit with her about what was happening in the neighborhood, but I couldn't have that woman lecturing me on my non-existent love life for not another minute. I was ready to go home to Bert and Ernie, then get Chris comfortable in his new pot.

"Of course you would know. I know Tokyo Valentine loves it when you get paid."

"I'm not even gonna ask how you know about that. Please just get out of my car," I huffed, the stress of the night making me hot.

Once I got Granny settled, I took a minute to figure out what I was going to eat from the safety of the driveway. I bought groceries and light snacks, but those weren't for tonight. Tonight I needed something bad for me. Something to soothe the sting of my only living relative basically calling me an incel. I finally settled on burgers, and I was off to midtown for the night, but as I pulled out of the driveway, I noticed someone backing into theirs.

A bright pink beetle reversed over a crisp pile of leaves with alarming speed, only to stop right before it could tap the

garage.
I couldn't see the driver since the windows were tinted, but for some reason, I was stuck. That house had belonged to a cantankerous veteran who let snakes thrive in the high grass when I was a kid, and now the property seemed well manicured and full of life. There was even a tree in the front yard. A tree full of fruit. Peaches to be exact. Perfectly round, unquestionably juicy peaches that practically appeared to be painted. The warm oranges and soft pinks felt triumphant amongst the autumn landscape. Especially since the evening was cooling down. The wind blew and one small fruit swayed in the gentle breeze. Suddenly my mouth watered for a taste of one. How long had it been since I ate a peach?

"BRRRRRNNNN."
The person behind me honked their horn, and the obnoxious, grating sound snapped me back to reality. The reality where I was basically canvasing a stranger's yard. Not only was I being creepy, but I was also being rude since the car behind me belonged to Granny's longtime neighbor, Ms. Aida, who just so happened to be on her way to her weekly game of spades. I knew she was calling me everything but a child of god for blocking the street. I don't know why spades made my people act up, but I quickly got on my way. The last thing I needed to add to my night was getting cussed out by somebody else's grandma after my own said I had no motion. No peach was worth that. I'd just have to get one from Publix next time.

Ermias

"I think someone stole my peach."
I slipped off my gloves then stood with a grumble to investigate Luci's claim. My wife stood four feet behind our peach tree, with the evening sun beaming on her cheekbones and the hem of her cotton sundress fluttering in the autumn wind. For a second I got distracted, but then I saw her frown. Right, back to business. We were talking about a peach. A peach on the tree. Luci's peach. And not the one hanging off her back.

The tree was pushing out its last harvest of the year, with certain leaves transitioning from bright green to simmering red.
"What peach?" I asked after carefully surveying the tree. Everything appeared intact to me. We were late into the harvest season but there was still plenty of fruit left. So much fruit that the branches practically hit a gangsta lean every time the breeze blew, and there were no damaged leaves from what I could tell.

"There was a little one on the left branch closest to the gate. I was waiting to see if it would get bigger," Luci grumbled.
"And you sure it wasn't a squirrel?"
"No, because the squirrels are disrespectful. They just take a single bite and throw your shit on the ground. It's completely gone."
She wasn't lying about the disrespect. There'd be plenty of mornings when I came out to check the garden beds only to end up cussing and sweeping for an hour because the vermin left half-eaten tomatoes and peppers everywhere.

"That's true. Maybe it was a neighbor kid. If so, I'm not mad. They're about to be sugared down from Halloween candy in a few days," I shrugged.
"No Erm, I think it has something to do with that truck that was watching the house last week."
"Baby, I think that truck was just waiting to see if you were parking or going."
"Nuhuh," Luci said, shaking her head from side to side. "Whoever was in there had a weird energy. I know they stole my shit. I'm gonna use a redemption hex."

Lucianna was gone before I could protest, with the front door slamming aggressively behind her. I thought about going after her in case she accidentally hexed a child, but it was likely too late. She probably already gathered up her herbs and moon water. Besides, I still had to top off the mulch in the beds before it rained that evening. I kneeled to pull yet another strand of tough crabgrass from between the stones with a loud sigh. I didn't know why Luci was so obsessed with that truck. We had both seen it visiting the neighborhood a few times, mostly parking at Ms. Claudette's house. I wasn't worried about whoever it was, they were likely a relative or a friend of our neighbor, but Luci swore there was a different kind of energy vibrating from them. That was her witch intuition acting up.

I knew my wife was witchy when I married her, and that was something I would never ask her to change. Hell, I was once a certified non-believer, but after seeing Luci work her magic to navigate life, her power was undeniable. We got this house because Luci said a spell in front of her makeshift altar that we had at our tiny, cramped studio. Every time I wanted a promotion, we would light an incense and the ancestors would make it so. Luci had also never been bitten by a mosquito, which by all means should've been impossible considering we lived in the middle of Georgia. So maybe she was right about the truck and whoever was in it, but for some reason, my intuition told me that it wasn't something to be worried about. Quite the opposite actually. My intuition told me I should be excited. Good things were about to happen.

M aia

It was so damn good.
Actually, scratch that. It was the best. The little peach I got off of the tree in my grandmother's neighbor's yard was the best thing I'd ever eaten, and I was pissed that I tried it. I walked past their gate one night on the way back to my car after dropping off snacks for Granny's book club when I saw it swaying in the wind. It glistened with rain while it bobbed up and down like a golden pendulum against the stormy, Southern, evening sky, and before I could realize what I was doing, I had plucked it from the branch and hurried away with it. At first I thought about returning it, but then I realized how weird that conversation would be.
"Yes, hi. I was watching your house from my car and then I

ended up stealing from you a couple days later. Would you like this back?"

Naw. Hell naw. That left me with no choice but to eat it. I had to get rid of the evidence, and to do anything else other than eat it would be not only a crime, but a sin. So I took a nibble hoping to find it under-ripe and grainy, but unfortunately it wasn't. The subtle tartness of the fuzzy skin, the tender, sweet, and sticky inner flesh, and the juice dribbling down my chin made for the most perfect first bite. The way I devoured it afterwards was obscene. I even ran my tongue across the pit, hoping to lap up any lingering sweetness there, then I moaned when I did. It had ruined me. Now I knew how delicious autumn peaches could be, even if they were stolen.

It had been a week since I'd eaten it, and I couldn't stop dreaming about it. Literally dreaming about it. The peach haunted me. Sometimes I'd get a phantom reminder of its delectable taste dancing on my tongue, other times I was subjected to the torturous task of watching myself eat it, a constant reminder of how I took the experience for granted. Other times I'd see flashes of myself in passing windows, my lips wet from the juice of the memory of the fruit. My appetite was ruined whenever that happened. It didn't matter what I had plans to eat. All I could think about was that fucking peach.

So it shouldn't have surprised me that the peach made an appearance in my dreams when I laid down on the second Friday before Halloween. It haunted me during the day, and night time was more opportune. The visions were much more vivid when I was too tired to distinguish imagination from reality. However, this time was different. There were people waiting for me in the shadows of my mind, and they were holding my peach. Well, their peach. *They knew* that I had stolen it, and they were going to make me pay for it. But not with money. Money wasn't enough for such an egregious offense.

Their nefarious grins cut through the darkness as they stepped forward with the damning evidence. I had saved the pit with the intent to try and replicate the expectational taste. My gluttony was my downfall, and I gasped as rough, heavy hands partnered with supple delicate ones to probe the entirety of my body. The calloused set traced me gently, but the soft ones were squeezing all of my curves and greedily sinking into every hole. My body melted into the bliss of near-ly-scalding warmth as I came closer to completion, only for my already-tense nerves to be shocked by something wicked-ly frigid. Hot and cold, rough and soft, my torture continued

in an endless loop until I was finally freed from them by the jarring ringing of my alarm. I sprang forward from the sheets with sweat dotting my brow, courtesy of my pounding heart. My damn bonnet was sliding down the wall beside me, and while I knew I went to bed alone, I expected to see the hands responsible for my ruin standing over me.
Except it really was just a dream.

T hat dream left me shaken for the rest of the morning, all the way through my thirty minute commute to the range. I knew vivid dreams were a thing but I never had them, and when I did have a scarily realistic dream, it was mostly about going to the toilet. If I was still religious, I would probably be worried about a sex demon. But I was doubtful that I was being plagued by an incubus since giving up white Jesus. An incubus would've at least let me get my nut off. So this was something else. I was being haunted, tortured, and straight up edged. I felt like...
"I'm cursed. I think," I confessed with a gulp.

Heavy silence followed my admission. Was that the best way to answer the phone at 9AM? Probably not. But if there was anyone I could talk to about this, it was her.
"Hello?" I whispered softly. "Did you hear me?"
"Yeah," Daya sighed. "I was trying to merge but now I'm stuck in traffic. I'm not gonna get to the Glendale branch for an hour. Fucking LA. Now hold up. Why do you think you're cursed exactly?"

Here I was, bothering my successful, educated, and busy best friend with my conspiracy theory bullshit. Because of that, I knew that I should absolutely not answer magical sex peaches, but what else was I supposed to say? I had burned a battery out in a wand since I ate that damn thing. I didn't know what else it could be. If it wasn't the peach, it sure as hell wasn't the gun powder and dry conversations with mediocre firearm enthusiasts.
"I stole something," I sighed.
Quiet came again, but before I got paranoid enough to interrupt it, Daya broke into amused laughter.

"Girl, no you didn't. What did you steal? Somebody's boyfriend?"

To be fair her reaction was completely warranted. My anxiety was too bad for me to steal. Hell, I even took a tomato back to get rang up once when the clerk missed it. Yet somehow I had the audacity to steal a peach from the house on the corner of Clarendon.

"No, Day. I'm being for real. I stole something out my grandma's neighbor's yard."

"Maia, what the hell? Ms. Claudette is gonna whoop you," Daya gasped. "What did you even take?"

"A peach."

"Wait, like an actual peach?"

"Yeah," I sighed.

"Girl, what in the Nurse Ratched?" Daya howled. "You stole a fucking peach?"

"Day, stop laughing!" I groaned. "This is serious."

"I bet it is, Peach Poacher. Who the fuck steals fruit? Are we in the middle ages?"

"Listen, it's a long story. I really didn't even mean to take it. I only realized it was in my hand when I was halfway home."

The line went quiet once again, but this time Daya's tone returned stern and rigid, like a clairvoyant grandmother.

"Bitch, burn some dirt. You probably are cursed. Who knows what kinda Juju they put on that shit."

"Do you think dirt will work or do I need to find a hoodoo lady?"

"I don't know, Mai. Shadow work ain't nothing to be played with. A lot of practitioners won't touch other people's karma curses. There's always a chance it could backfire on them, especially if the cursed knows what they did wrong."

"Are you sure your grann doesn't have anything for stuff like this? Doesn't she do voodoo?"

"I mean yeah, but she's all the way in Haiti. Plus again, you were in the wrong. Po Po ain't gone touch that."

"So what do I do?" I gulped as the feeling of doom settled into my stomach.

"Go apologize and offer amends," Daya said firmly. "Witches are only vindictive to a point."

"Amends? Like a chicken or something?"

"Girl, hell naw!" Daya scoffed. "Some money or something. What the hell are you on?"

"Don't yell at me!" I moaned. "I'm worried. I ain't never pissed a witch off before."

"Well there's a first time for everything," she huffed. "Let me know how it goes."

Ermias

I had time off for the first time in seven months. Exactly two weeks off.
The average person would be stressed the fuck out to work seven days straight for seven months, but I was lucky to be doing what I loved. My grandparents were both master gardeners when I was growing up which inspired my love of plants. When I found out you could get a college degree in botany and horticulture my fate was sealed. My mom was worried I wouldn't make any money digging in the dirt all the time but I stayed at it anyway, and now I was the head landscaper for Atlanta's Botanical Garden. I could trick on my little treat, pay my bills, and do what I loved.
Life was good.
I just missed my other interests on occasion.

Lucianna had portable hobbies: knitting, sketching, and reading. Hobbies that you could pick up at any time, almost anywhere and still do them effectively. Meanwhile I had hobbies that required total concentration for extended periods of time. Hobbies like baking and range practice.

I had a membership to a black-owned range that was in Decatur. It had been open for around 3 or 4 years but I had only been there twice. Once to get my membership, and about three months after that when they hosted one of the night owl sessions. The owner was a self proclaimed reformed night owl who occasionally still dabbled in midnight activities, and I was eternally grateful to her because that was the only night in the last almost-year I could squeeze my practice time in.

I had never met the owner of Shoot Sharp, but I was strangely intrigued by her. The staff had nothing but praise for her, they were compensated fairly and seemed to enjoy their jobs. Apparently she was also very involved in the community, often donating supplies and time. Plus she was one of the few accredited Mark Smiths in the state, *and* she just so happened to be a black woman. Black women were so vastly underrepresented in the field that Miss Mamas automatically got tens across the board from me.

Yet I didn't want to meet her just in case she somehow failed to live up to the hype. I was easily irked by most people and I couldn't handle that kind of disappointment if she were to fall into that category. I was hopelessly delusional when it came to beautiful women, especially the smart ones. I spent my whole life surrounded by smart women and it was my default to treat them like they were God's gift to earth even if they were hell in pretty packaging. That was why it took me six months to ask Luci out. She was too beautiful to be real, and emotional risk taking was not my specialty, especially then. Nothing much had changed in five years. I asked Luci out of course, but I was still a delusional cynic. So meeting Maia Hill on purpose was out of the question.

However, the universe had other plans. As I exited the recently bleach and fabuloso sanitized bathroom, I bumped right into the elusive woman who was backing out of her office with a phone clutched against her neck.
"Shit, my bad," I said, catching her waist.
I grabbed her because she was going to hit the floor if I hadn't. However in the second she was clutched against my chest, I was hit with a pleasant wave of frankincense and vanilla. It was an uncommon combination but it worked for her. She smelled so good I almost didn't want to let her go. But when my palm grazed her exposed belly, she jumped back and into a wall like I had electrocuted her. Her head bumped the adjoining door with a sickening thud.

"Are you ok?" I said, bringing my hand to my mouth in shock. If I hadn't recently cleaned my glasses, I would've questioned if I accidentally stabbed her with how she glared at me.
"Yeah. I'm cool," she nodded while rubbing her scalp. "Sorry, you seem familiar. Have we met before?"

My eyes went out of focus for a split second while I processed her question. Too much was happening at once. She was bumping into walls, asking me shit, and I was trying hard not to stare at the racing hills and sensuous valleys of her curves despite my body's protest. If I had met a woman like her before, I would've definitely remembered. And yet I still struggled to produce an answer.
"No," I said slowly. "I don't think so."
Her eyes sparkled with curiosity as she watched me speak, and in that moment I knew for damn sure we hadn't met before. I could never forget a woman like that, and so far I never had. However sure I was though, she still didn't seem convinced.

"I'm Maia," she supplied expectantly.
"Ermias," I gulped.
We watched each other in the hall for God knows how long. When Luci told me she wanted me to consider polyamory, I had trouble picturing *truly* loving anyone else. Sure I could lay with another woman, but would I appreciate the unevenness of her complexion, or the subtle display of nerves in her wrought hands, or the way her wild, untamed curls licked the nape of neck? Up until now I always thought the answer would be no.
But then I met Maia.
Tall, beautiful, nervous, Maia.

"Maia?" the desk attendant called. "Are you still in your office? Your class is about to start."

Whatever magic brewing between us in the moment was turned flat as Maia remembered that she had places to be. Her eyes dulled with the return of routine, but a little sparkle remained when she flashed me a polite smile.

"I should get going, but thank you, Ermias," she cooed.

"No problem," I nodded.

"See you around?"

"Definitely," I hummed, sounding every bit mannish as I was currently behaving.

I watched shamelessly while Maia's long, moisturized legs carried her around the corner, leaving me where I stood outside of her office. Dazed, confused, and a little hopeful.

Luci was right about magic feeling tingly.

Chapter 3

Future Vision

Lucianna

"Luci, I met a lady!" Ermias announced, busting through the front door.

I was halfway through the newest Ducati Mob release when Erm came home. It had been on my Kindle all week, teasing me whenever I had a little too much free time. I told myself I'd spend all day with it to make up for all the other missed opportunities.

But then my husband met a woman.

"Oh deets!" I shrieked, climbing over the arm of the couch and making Erm frown.

As benevolent as Ermias was, he hated when I did that. His grandparents' influence on his life was far-reaching, and that included furniture preservation. If he had it his way, we'd have plastic on the sofa.

"I'm going to ignore the way you just disrespected my couch for the sake of getting this all out," he started. "But it was kind of serendipitous. She's actually the owner of the range and it was my first time meeting her."

"The owner of Shoot Sharp? You tryna get a free membership or something?" I teased.

"Pfft, please. You know how I feel about free stuff."

"Yes I know," I sighed. "It's one of the few things I don't appreciate about you."

Ermias didn't believe anything was truly free. He believed you would pay some kind of price in some kind of way. Meanwhile if it was free, it was for me.

"But go on. Tell me more," I urged. "What did she look like?"

"Whew, let's sit down," Erm suggested. "It's a lot."

I listened to him talk about a five minute interaction for 30 minutes straight. It was necessary though, because the way he described her flawless coffee complexion, bright eyes, and generous bust had me salivating. I was so enamored that I

even tried to get him to drive back to the range, but Ermias reminded me how creepy it would be to interrupt that lady's business to gawk at her.
Unfortunately he was right.

"So are you gonna get her number?" I asked while chewing on my thumb nail.
Nail biting was a habit I had long abandoned, especially when I got grown enough to afford regular maintenance with acrylic and gel polish. However, the potential connection made me anxious. Me and Ermias had been flirting with the idea of a third partner for years. However, we almost never had the same taste in women. I wanted someone more like Erm, and he wanted someone more like me. I hadn't met Maia but a quick Google search had my heart thumping. She seemed like the perfect blend of both of our personalities, and God was she beautiful. The creator did overtime on her. Pretty somehow didn't do her justice.

"Stop that, Luc," Erm chided while gently lowering my hand. "I'm gonna get her number, but it'll probably take me a minute. You know I only got a few days off and I got stuff I need to do around here. Plus we got that Halloween party next Friday and we still haven't gotten costumes."
"Oh yeah I forgot about that," I grimaced. "Are you sure I can't just dust off some old lingerie?"
"Luci, please don't tempt me," Erm growled while pulling me into his lap. "You promised you'd behave this week." "Did I?" I simpered as his calloused hands carefully scraped against the skin of my inner thighs.
"You did."
"It must've slipped my mind," I purred while straddling Ermias' wide lap.
"Just like how putting panties on slipped your mind?" he asked while tracing my outer lips.

I never wore panties. Yeah I owned them, but they were reserved for temperatures below 35 degrees, periods, and long walks. Fat ma needed to air out, and while going commando had its pros, it also had its cons. A con being how easy it was for my thin skort to become noticeably soaked after enduring Ermias' manipulation, yet the pro was much the same. His erection came to rest against the agonizingly thin gusset of my shorts where he made it jump twice for good measure.
"Remind me what I was supposed to be doing again?" I pleaded.
"Behavin," Ermias grunted while stroking my hardened nipples.

Erm loved to play with me, but when my moans were no longer teasing and light, his hand slipped between my legs to remove the barrier between us. With my shorts pushed to the side, he raised up slightly to free his dick from his joggers. The hoe in me got excited. We hadn't fucked with clothes on in ages. I just knew I was about to get treated like a motel whore.

"You need a reminder on how to act right, Lucianna?" Erm asked as he drew my lips between his.

The kiss was just as coaxing as his question. My immediate answer was yes, full stop. However I knew it would be better if I made him work for it.

"I am acting right," I pouted. "It's three in the afternoon and I still have clothes on."

Ermias' hungry gaze traveled from the stolen, haphazardly buttoned dress shirt down to the short, flirty skirt that I couldn't comfortably bend over in. His pointer finger and thumb then carefully worked to unfasten the buttons standing in between himself and my needy nipples. My shirt fell open carelessly, allowing him to graze the sensitive skin of my areolas with his fingertips.

"Tease," I whimpered.

"I prefer the term seducer," Erm corrected while his touch traveled across the planes of my belly and thighs.

He was always gentle despite his rough, heavy hands. That was true even as used his grip on my ass to impale me on his angry dick, and it was especially true when he held my chin to kiss me.

It was almost cruel considering how hard he fucked me.

"I don't know, Luc. She was pretty, but this is still the best pussy I'll ever have," Erm moaned while burying himself in me.

"That's cause we haven't tried Maia's yet," I sighed.

I could practically taste her lips in my lucid state. It was as if seeing her had unlocked long-forgotten memories of our past and dreams of our future. Memories of warm nights and slow, intentional mornings shared between the three of us. I wanted her bad.

"It might be good but it's not beating yours," Ermias cooed while nuzzling me.

We had moved from the couch over to the recliner and Erm was using the swivel rock feature to his utmost advantage. I knew I had another point to make, but I lost my mental outline as our hips circled like a wreath with the assistance of the chair beneath us. I understood why Erm crowned me the pussy queen. My shit was sloppy-wet and scorching hot.

"Bet five on it," I said finally when my mind landed back on

Maia.

"On what?" Ermias grumbled.

"I bet five that Maia has some of the best pussy you or I have ever had. Right up there with mine."

"Shittt," he grunted while deepening his strokes. "I'll bet twenty on it. I'm confident in my kitty kat. Look at how sweetly she purrs for me."

"Be that as it may, I know what I'm talking about here. I'm a connoisseur."

"Ok, coochie connoisseur. We'll see. Just let me finish up with my current plate first."

"Yes please," I laughed as his arms wrapped around me. "Give me that act right."

Maia

Again.
I snapped my eyes back towards the vanity in front of me. I was alone in my bathroom, and yet I could smell perfume and hear laughter.
Her laughter.
It was pleasing and resounding. Still feminine but not at all delicate or airy. Then somehow it was familiar. Familiar enough to inspire me to smile despite the fact that it was disconnected from the person. I smiled every single time I heard it. Even though I should've been terrified of it marking the end of my mental stability.

Lots of folklore suggested that October was a transitional lapse between the spirit world and ours. That those darker and colder days made it easier for spirits to slip through the veil and cause chaos on this side. I thought it was an interesting theory, but I never paid it much mind until now. Now though, I had no choice but to reevaluate my stance on ghouls, ghosts, and witches because I had pissed one off.

She had haunted me since, refusing the money I left in the mailbox for my committed transgression. Instead she sought payment in my dreams, my nightmares, and my memories. When I cooked breakfast I knew she preferred her eggs over medium with salt and pepper, and her pancakes with apple butter. When I laid down she told me that she had been waiting on me to mess up. And when I finally snapped out of my mirror delusions and climbed in the shower, she reminded me that it'd take two lifetimes for me to repay what I had stolen.

Her hands were just as greedy then as they were the first night, grabbing handfuls of whatever she could with her phantom touch. My hands pressed against the shower walls for balance as her lips fell up my collar. Then I felt it again. Dangerously hot and freezing cold. I wanted to believe it was just my imagination, possibly even my hormones, but sweat slicked my skin when she kissed me, and goosebumps followed when she moved away. My head spun from the conflicting sensations, and I was so dizzy with frustration that I practically had to crawl back into my room when I was done.

I flung my towel into the hamper, just barely catching the rim, and then rushed to pull open the third drawer on the left. Usually I was elated to have multiple pairs of clean socks at my disposal, but today they just pissed me off. After a second too long for my liking, I finally located my favorite ride, a massive baby-pink corn cob dildo and an accompanying bullet. It was the type of thing you buy after a night of drinking and doom scrolling. One of the things that made me question if I should really be trusted with adult money. The answer? Probably not. But that didn't matter right then because I was mere moments away from backing against any hard surface like a cat in heat.

I rocked slowly at first, allowing myself time to adjust to the girth. I actually bought this one because it reminded me of Angel, and it was the best I could get to the real thing on the regular since he and Velma were still living their best Orlando lives. They were only six hours away in light traffic but it still wasn't close enough for regular visits. I missed my friends. I missed us all living in an arms reach, and I especially missed having regular socialization and freaky ass sex. Especially when all ten of us got together, and especially when Dolly brought her strap. I let my memories of our last trip replay in my mind as I slipped further down the cob and let it stretch me. Visions of courtyard cunnilingus guided me to the precipice of my first orgasm, and recollections of Daya's ass, mouth, and pussy getting stretched out threw me into my next one.

I could hardly remember to breathe as I filled myself, and while most of it could be attributed to my memories, some of it was because of the feeling of Ermias' lingering gaze on my ass. I remembered how his smile curved when I turned the corner, and suddenly, I broke. I rode faster and harder, letting my ass bang against the hardwood and shake the whole room. The muscles in my thighs had to give out before I convinced myself to slow down, and even then my pussy was still spasming over the length of the cob, wringing my body for everything it had.

I collapsed in a small puddle of my own mess after finally catching my breath. My chin was resting on the floor while my legs were bent to resemble a bullfrog. That was such a good nut. Such a hard-earned one too.
Yet when I smelled the familiar phantom scent of white amber and musk, my hand was back in between my legs rubbing circles over my poor, tortured clit.
"This is fucking nasty," I mumbled, although I was unwilling to stop.

Abusing my pussy was my life now.
I had scheduled my vacation for this week so I could go to the party, and ever since I got off on Wednesday night, my fingers and whatever toy I had in reach had been lodged inside of me. I knew libido ramped up with age for most women, but this was just ridiculous. There were things I needed to get done,

calls I needed to make. How was I supposed to do any of that when my coochie wept every time the wind blew?

I wanted to blame the witch again, but this was all that man's fault. The fine brown-skinned one at the range.
Ermias.
I'd seen him pop in once before and I thought he was handsome then, but I didn't make a habit out of interrupting people's free time. Especially not members, and especially not men. I had worked too hard for too long to let something as ubiquitous as dick take me to hell. Yet this particular man had me rethinking everything. It was crazy. I couldn't remember what all happened in that hall, but I could remember every cell in my body lit ablaze as soon as he touched me. Meanwhile he was probably somewhere rubbing his feet together, completely oblivious as to what he'd done to me. Hell, he might not even remember me aside from his minor admiration. We were perfect strangers.

In any other instance I'd be embarrassed to project my insatiable horniness onto a stranger, but I knew it was his fault for some gut-deep reason. Those hazel eyes trapped me in a honey jar the second I met them with my own. Plus it didn't help that the roughness of his grip reminded me of the haunting sex dream I kept having. Even his chuckle landed with a certain undeniable familiarity. Everything about meeting him felt like a carefully planned coincidence. A coincidence I'd probably question on any other day.

But tonight I needed to stop daydreaming about wetting his perfectly curly beard and manage to leave my pussy alone long enough to get dressed up.
Tonight was for celebration.
I remembered wanting to dress up as Star Fire for Halloween as a kid and showing Granny the comic inspiration with excitement coursing through my veins only to be shot down immediately. Granny Girl rarely denied me outfits or hairdos for being "too grown" but OG 80s Star Fire was a hard no. As an adult with adult money and free will, I now understood her reasoning. A deeeep v-cut purple sequined unitard was indeed too grown for eight-year-old me. Thirty-three-year-old me, however? Yeah, we had that shit on. The hair, the boots, the way my titties were just barely contained in the thin straps of the halter. It was all perfection. If I was looking for someone to take home, I knew for sure I'd have no problem finding them. However, that didn't matter to me right then. I just wanted to show up for myself and remember that I was a bad bitch, partner or not.

Chapter 4

Trance

I hadn't been to a weekend Halloween party in ages, let alone a Halloween party in general. As costumed patrons flocked the entrances, I remembered why they were so fun. Where else were you going to see Big Bird jigging with The Koolaid Man? 90s Halloween jams poured out from every window. The mansion Sam rented for the occasion was decked out in wispy webs, leggy spiders, and phantom holographs, then the front lawn was littered with expressive skeletons while a mysterious fog occluded the perimeter. There were bright motion sensor lanterns posted near the parking spots for arriving guests to safely maneuver their vehicles, but everything beyond that was dark and spooky.
Perfectly on theme.

I only took a second to adjust my tits, making sure that I wouldn't have a nip slip as I walked up the dramatic flared steps to the festivities. The air smelled warm and nostalgic, like spiced rum cider, kettle corn, and fried fare food. It was finally cooling off in Georgia so I appreciated the cider most of all, and I also regretted ever missing out on it along with everything else. Especially Sam. Me and Sam never bumped cooters, but she was still one of my pillars all through college and young adulthood. We understood each other and there was never any judgement. Yet as soon as shit didn't work out for me and I felt exposed, I pulled away. It was a shitty thing to do but I just wanted to lick my wounds in peace. Samara didn't hold it against me though. She still greeted me at the door like she did all the years previous, all smiles and wide eyes.

"Maiaaaaa," she sang while pulling me into a hug. "Look at the hair, your titties sitting all nice. I can't believe you came. Oh my God. I feel like I'm witnessing the return of the prodigal son."
"Sammy, don't be dramatic," I chuckled.
"No, I'm serious! I missed you so much. I knew you needed

your space to figure everything out, but I was hoping you'd come back eventually."
My heart squeezed. Part of me assumed Sam was just sending me invitations out of decency all those years. I didn't think she actually missed my presence.

"Thank you, baby girl," I cooed. "I promise not to crash out and suck dick on the band stage this year."
"Shit, you can if you want," she shrugged. "That nigga deserved to be embarrassed and lots of people there that night left with great tips. I for one finally figured out how to do that tongue thing."
"Sam!" I gasped. "Is that why you and Vic were announcing a baby by February?"
"Maybeeee," she giggled. "All I know is I want a memoir some-day when you finally settle down. I need full-time mentorship so I can keep affording these parties."
"Girl, please," I chuckled. "Vic adores you. He's gonna get you whatever you want regardless of what that mouth do."
"Yeah but my mouth doing the tongue thing helps."
"Touché," I nodded, dropping my voice an octave. "It definite-ly doesn't hurt."
"Alright Mai," Sam chortled before waving me off. "Go have fun. I'll be here all night but you know they be snatching up the rum."
"Heard," I said while locating a dispenser. "See you later on."

Lucianna

I hadn't played for a crowd since we moved three years ago. It was as intoxicating as I remembered it to be though. Every strum synchronized with my pounding heart. The rhythm flooded my veins right along with the adrenaline, and the crowd was just as mesmerizing. Everyone either clapped or stomped along to my riff, and although I knew it was hella corny, I kneeled on stage underneath the spotlight at the bridge so that I didn't have to focus on anything but my fu-riously moving hands. My fingertips had softened from disuse so I didn't have my once familiar callouses to protect me as I plucked the strings, but that didn't matter. All that mattered was the echo of my guitar and the swaying of the myriad of hips in front of me. We had a full house and we were killing it. *I* was really killing it.

"Whew!!! Luci's still got it!" Sam cheered, bringing her ap-plauding hands overhead.
"You know I could never lose it," I chuckled while curtseying. "The ancestors said I'm her, so I had no choice but to do this shit."
"Well I'm grateful," Vic added. "Ole boy backed out at the

last minute and we almost didn't have a band. You know Sam waits all year to dance at these shits. So thanks for helping out tonight."

"Anytime," I smiled. "Especially since I was promised free top shelf for me and Erm all night?" I asked in confirmation.

"Have at it," Vic chuckled. "I wouldn't have been able to afford you without it."

"That is absolutely not true. I'd do anything for Sam."

Vic's eyebrows shot up into his forehead. I could see the businessman in him warring with his loverboy side. Of course he wanted Sam happy, but Erm was about to decimate all the brown liquor, and he now knew the cost for my last minute services could've been less.

Oh well! I believed in the universal rule of no takesies-backsies.

"Sorry no refunds," I teased as I sauntered to the bar for a sidecar. "Next time feel free to ask about the friends and family discount!"

Ermias was already waiting on me with a chilled drink when I got back to my stool. It was the perfect cognac color to ease me into the festivities, and the sugar rim was the cherry on top. I took a slow sip, realized it was Hennessey, and then panicked.

"Wait, you didn't pay for this did you?"

"No, Luci," Erm chuckled. "Vic told the bar to comp our drinks as soon as Sam asked you. He knew you'd say yes."

"I gotta stop being so damn predictable," I grumbled as I took another calming sip.

"Lady, please. You're hardly predictable. I still can't believe you gave all this up."

I let my glasses slip down to my nose to glare at him while I took another sip . When me and Erm first met, I was on the road as a lead guitarist for the band, Infalliable. As our relationship developed, I slowly lost interest in the rock star life. Instead I found something more stable and flexible, and transitioned into a career in audio post-production and engineering. Part of him still believed that he ruined some great American dream for me when in reality, he was my dream. I regretted nothing. Except wearing panties tonight.

"You hush," I chided. "I didn't give up anything. I outgrew that scene. I prefer being home on Tuesday nights, watching you check the soil pH."

"pH night does get kinda wild," he chuckled while pulling my seat close. "But baby, we both know you could be playing for sold-out crowds in sparkly thongs."

"Ermias, please. We both know I hate underwear."

"Speaking of underwear," he growled. "I hope you have some on under that dress."

I had on underwear simply because the temperature had fallen below my threshold for mini-dresses. Contrary to popular belief hoes did get cold, and I had no intention of letting Jack Frost blow his wintery-ass breath up my snatch. But it was better to keep Erm wondering. Wonder inspired want.
"Maybe," I shrugged. "You can find out later, but right now I owe the drum guy an autograph. Let me do my rounds and I'll be back."
"Ok, baby. I'll be waiting," he replied with a soft kiss.
I turned to scoot off my spinning stool and Ermias lost to his impulse, giving me a gentle pat on the ass as I walked off.
Social obligations aside, I was excited about where the night would lead us. Because after Ermias knocked me out for the night it would be tomorrow. Tomorrow meant we would talk to Maia.

M aia

I couldn't remember the last time I heard a guitar sound so sultry. Goosebumps raced across my arms and chest every time I heard a new string. It might've been the rum, but something told me the alcohol swimming in my stomach wasn't the only contributor to the reaction I had when the band was on stage.
No, tuition told me it was actually *her*.

The lead guitarist, Lucianna. At least that's the name her bandmates introduced when she climbed onto the stage. She was dressed as the queen of hearts, but she was the embodiment of sin in my mind. A short, curvy, gum-drop button of a woman with wild hair, animated eyes, and wondrously gifted hands. Despite the pretty caramel-brown face accompanying them, her hands were what I stared at during her entire performance. The fixation was just as shocking as it was unfounded. Her hands looked completely normal except for a few tattoos wrapped around her knuckles, and yet I couldn't look away. I was like a cobra in a flute trance, mindlessly swaying my life away to the machinations of a stranger.

It didn't get better once she got off the stage either. I knew better than to seek her out because any femme who could play guitar like that would definitely ruin my life. Yet visions of her kneeling on stage like an anointed prophet swarmed my mind. I wasn't optimistic enough to believe in love at first sight, but she *almost* had my ass. Especially when she bumped into me at the cider station.

"Shit, I am so sorry," she rushed out as our drinks spilled. "I wasn't watching where I was going an-"

We made eye contact and Lucianna suddenly stopped talking. Her mouth curled into a silent O, then the fiery gaze I previously saw on stage reignited as her eyes landed on my liquor-soaked titties.

At least I knew she was gay.

I felt a little better about lusting after her, knowing that she was gay.

"It's ok," I said, offering her my hand. "You're Lucianna right? I'm Maia."

At first she just mugged me and I thought I did something wrong, but after I gave her an awkward smile, I watched as Lucianna gave me a slow nod in agreement.

"Ni-nice to meet you, Maia. Call me Luci."

I nodded back and then we just stood there staring at each other. I was acutely aware of how weird it must've looked to the people around us, but that wasn't enough to make me stop. The expression "easy on the eyes" finally made sense to me. Pretty somehow didn't seem like an accurate description for her. Breathtaking could get the job done, but it was somehow still missing a vital piece that had to be so uniquely Lucianna. It didn't account for her grit or the slight air of magic surrounding her. Captivating was more like it.

"I just wanted to say that you killed that shit on stage," I chuckled softly, finally breaking our silence.

"Thank you," she smiled while also snapping out of her daze. "I'm sorry for spilling on you. I can remove the stains though if you want. I keep that thang on me."

She dried me off with a wad of paper towels then pulled open the zipper of her fanny pack and produced a large Tide pen that was ready for action. However this fabric was dry clean only, and in all honesty, I had plans to have my seamstress convert it into lingerie after tonight was done.

"It's no big deal," I shrugged. "I get costumes anticipating that there will be stains if the night goes right."

"Smart lady," she conceded with a tilt of her curly head.

"Most times," I laughed.

I generally believed I was smart, but right then I felt dumb as fuck. I could barely shut my mouth to keep from drooling over her. My hands itched to trace the tattoos adorning her arms and chest. Hell, my hands itched to trace her everywhere. Then she had to go and make it worse by putting her hand on my arm.

She gave me a beat of cool, controlled laughter that sounded so familiar yet so foreign, I had heard it before, I was sure of it, but I just couldn't quite place where. I almost started to panic because the weird sensation was back. The electrifying, hair-raising buzz I felt when that man, Ermias, caught me in the hall. At first I thought I was tripping, but as Lucianna's fingers settled onto my forearm I knew my initial reaction to be accurate. My mind slipped from reality into a twisted vision of her kneeling before me, but it was gone when I blinked. Something strange was happening, and I was more than sure that they were at the center of it.

"Can I buy you a drink to replace the first one?" Luci asked softly.
Her question snapped me out of my manic spiral. I was back in reality, yet I was still unable to speak. So I just gave her a silent nod and then followed her towards the bar, hand in hand. The buzzing was still present, and while it was creating a mess of my mind, I had come down from my delusions. The chances of Ermias and Luci knowing each other with a city as dense as Atlanta were slim to none. I met Ermias at the range in Decatur and now I was partying in a mansion over in Vinnings.
The woozy, love-struck feeling was just coincidental.
That or I really really needed to get some ass.

Speaking of asses, Luci had a nice one. Her shape kind of reminded me of Velma and Hen's. Her ass was double wide while her bust and shoulders were petite. She had perfect little handfuls of boob. She really didn't even need to wear a bra.
"What are you drinking?" Luci asked as we approached the bar.
See, men got in trouble for ogling women because they didn't have the decency nor the good sense to stop during conversation. Women on the other masked their perverted intentions. We could be thinking about six different ways to fold ya and still prioritize human decency. So I had met Luci's eyes when she started talking to me, even though I was still wholly thinking about her titties.

"Who, me?" I squawked.
"Yeah Mai–tai, who else?" she giggled.
It was rare that I accepted a nickname. So far in my life it had

only happened twice, once with Granny, and once with Daya. One of those people was my guardian and last living relative, and the other had been by my side my entire adult life, even after I called her at 7am West Coast time to cry about being cursed. Yet the nickname given to me by a woman I met all of five minutes ago carried the same weight as both of those. Hearing her call me Mai-Tai made me happy.
Either this was actually love at first sight or that cider was whooping my ass this year.

"I'll just have a sidecar," I sighed, trying to shake the undue affection out of my voice.
"Ooh, that's my favorite," Luci grinned, bringing it right back. "Two sidecars, please!"
I assumed she had a tab running which is why she only handed the bartender a crisp $5 for the drinks. Yet watching her collect our glasses prompted me to observe other things about her. Things like her vintage, probably thrifted belt, the small smoking gun tattoo on her ankle, and her nails that were painted a sinful red with an accompanying black french tip. Her nails that coincidentally matched mine. The main differences being my colors inverted and given some gory red drips of blood to accentuate the Halloween theme.

"Hey we kind of match," Luci said, noticing my nails as she passed me my drink.
"I just noticed," I nodded while taking a skeptical sip. "Hey, where'd you get that belt?"
I'd seen belts like that at vintage resale shops and once at a big sale. Seeing her with one on made me wonder if we crossed paths before and didn't realize it.
"Oh this?" she asked while gripping one of the bronze loops. "I was at an estate sale out in Kennesaw and the lady had mad vintage stuff. You know how they were back in the day though, so I couldn't fit shit but the shoes and accessories."

Just as I suspected, I had gone to that same sale. But I only went on Sunday instead of Friday and Saturday.
"Oh my God, I was at that same sale. The clothes pissed me off so bad. They way I cried when I first found out Juicy Couture tracksuits were not made to fit actual juicy asses?" I sighed. "Embarrassing."
"Girl, tell me about it. Just false advertising. Let's find us a table."
That was all she had to say. It wasn't everyday I got to chat with a fellow thrift queen baddie.
Or the potential love of my life.

Lucianna

I should've felt bad. I really should've.
When Ermias first talked to me about Maia, I promised not to pursue her before we had a chance to approach her together. So when I saw her standing there, hair and makeup on point, with her long legs poking out from underneath a skirt that could only be classified as micro, I shouldn't have approached her. I definitely shouldn't have been sitting at a dimly lit booth with her, sharing a plate of random party appetizers and laughing about our memories of Sam, and some of the trash costumes we'd seen. Especially the myriad of interracial couples dressed as Mary and Stack. They had formed their own little community of corniness by the entrance, hoping to get a reaction from those coming and going. Me and Maia giggled every time someone scoffed at them. Her smile and laugh was now branded into the folds of my brain. So yes, technically I should've felt bad but circumstances prevented me from feeling anything but blessed.
Besides, I didn't pursue her. I accidentally spilled my drink on her and offered to make up for it.
There was a difference.
Albeit a small one.

Also, I was on my best behavior. I hadn't whispered in the shell of her ear, or trailed my fingers up her cushy thighs when she laughed a little too long, nor did I try to kiss her when she leaned in close to whisper something to me. I was being cool, calm, and collected and all was going well.
But then the beat dropped.

Sam loved opening and closing a party to a live band, but that didn't mean she was too cultured to play some ass shaking music. Chief Keef's Jam played over the speakers and Maia convinced me to knock back the rest of our drinks and hit the dance floor. What started with me throwing it in a circle quickly evolved into a watching crowd marvel at me and Maia as we twerked synchronously. Ass to ass, back to back, hands intertwined, our hips rocked along to the rhythmic bass. The small breeze flowing through the swinging door barely did anything to cool my feverish skin. Maia was just as hot, and as she pulled me close against her chest with the slowing tempo, I knew our heat was due to more than just dancing.

"I forgot how much fun these things were," she snorted as someone in a leather Shrek get-up, twerked in our absence.
"Been a while since you've been out?" I asked.
"Mhm. I had a bad break up so I took some time to myself," she nodded.
"Damn, I'm sorry. I know girl heartbreak is the worst."
Maia took a deep breath and then frowned into her drink like she was trying to wash the bad taste out of her mouth.

"Unfortunately it wasn't a girl. I probably would've been less pissy if it was."

Suddenly all my hopes clattered to the floor. We were vibing so well that I didn't even bother to inquire if she liked girls. Probably because the way she held me as we danced to Such A Thing screamed otherwise. It made sense though. Maia was a pretty ass stallion. Of course she wanted a big strong man to stand beside her and make her feel dainty. All I'd do next to her is look like a purse.

"I'm sorry," I choked out. "I didn't mean to assume. For whatever reason I just pictured you with a woman."
I pictured her with me, specifically. Us in coordinating pajamas and snuggling on Sundays while Ermias went to weed garden beds at the ass crack of dawn.
"Oh, don't apologize. I do like women," Maia shrugged. "I'm actually pan. I met my ex-fiance in college and I didn't figure out I was *really* gay until after we were already involved. But we were poly so it didn't really matter. Anddd I'm oversharing. Um, I'm sorry."

Her hands came to the hem of her skirt so she could wrap her fingers around the shiny fabric. For a second I mistakenly thought she was nervous. Women like Maia didn't get nervous.
Unless...
It took my dumb girl brain way too long to catch on to what was happening. Mostly because I was distracted by Maia's big ass titties. However I eventually realized that the ancestors were giving me an opening. I would have to grovel at Ermias' feet for a week, but damn it, I was taking it.

"You're not oversharing. I just told you I believed in the tooth fairy until I was 15. Besides, I'm poly too."
"Hey!" Maia smiled. "Look at us beating the stereotypes."
"Oh that all poly people are ugly? Who started that stereotype anyway?"
"I don't know but I can't stand it," Maia groaned while throwing her head back. "People start treating you like you musty if you tell them your poly."
"Nope, that Degree working overtime," I laughed after sniffing my pits. "I got a bath with my name on it after this."
"Me too," Maia sighed. "But I need to use the bathroom right quick. Do you wanna come with?"

Yes, yes, a thousand times yes. Of course I wanted to go with her. It only took me an hour to decide that I loved being near Maia. I wanted to watch her dance in the bathroom mirrors and reapply her lipstick. Or even just watch the bubbles glide over her hands. But I knew I was flying too close to the sun when I smiled like the joker while imagining either scenario. "No, go ahead and I'll come find you. I need to go check in with Sam about the closing."

"Ok, see you soon," she grinned.

"Yeah," I nodded, knowing I needed to go find Erm immediately. "See you soon."

Chapter 5

Rift

Ermias

Nothing beats a Jet2 holiday.
Except getting free drinks all night because your wife was a bad-ass rockstar. I was feeling great despite Luc leaving me to go socialize, but that continuous buzz came with a price. My bladder was screaming two hours in. I tried to hold off just in case Luc came looking for me, but that fourth Old Fashion popped up to collect its dues.

After squeezing past two Mega Minds and an Octopus, I found a urinal with my name on it. I felt lighter after unburdening myself, but panic started to set it because it took me way too long just to get everything out. I had a strange feeling that someone was looking for me. So I quickly scrubbed my hands, grabbed a few paper towels, and dipped. Well, more like shuffled. The hall was tight as hell with all the fabric from elaborate Halloween costumes. Everyone had to go. Sam served a spread every year plus the cider, delicious and complimentary which only contributed to the sprawling bathroom lines.

I had gotten in and out before it got too busy, but now I was stuck in traffic, waiting for the Big Bird and Elmo to scooch out the way. Folks were practically hugging the wall in an attempt to be courteous and make space. Which meant it was the perfect time for some drunk ass nigga in the back of the line to act up.
"Damn, can y'all start walking?" he screeched before trying to *push* his way through.

Part of the reason I preferred to work with plants instead of people was because of situations like this. People were a mixed bag. Some people had patience and common sense, but most didn't. I was already irritated because I could see the top of Luci's head as she floated through the crowds looking for me, and the hollering ass mother fucker behind me had horrible timing.

Then he really sealed the deal by pushing someone into me.

"Shit, I'm sorry," she said before turning to face the instigator. "Watch where the fuck you going, bitch ass nigga."

Actually he didn't just push anybody into me. He pushed Maia. *Our* Maia. She had on ten pounds of hair, a full face of makeup, and crazy contacts, but I'd recognized that backside bumping into me anywhere.

"Maia, are you ok?" I asked gently.

I was waving my hand around her BAPs wig trying to tuck any potential stray hairs back in place when the dude who was responsible for her unrighting added his two pissy-ass cents.

"She need to move the fuck out of the way," the man spat.

I almost broke my neck crooning to see who the fuck he was talking to. I could tell by the nut suffocaters he considered jeans that he was the YN type, but the only switches that scared me were the ones my granddaddy made me get off the tree.

Maia looked ready to go off, but I pushed her behind me before it could get too far.

"Say, young man. How about you slide the fuck on somewhere before you get handled?" I grinned.

"Nah I got something you can handle, twin," he barked back.

Just as I expected, he started reaching into his pants, but he wasn't gonna pull shit out them tight mother fuckers before I got to him. I allowed him just enough time to give him false hope before I artfully repositioned his head with the back of my hand. He fell to the floor without much fuss, splitting the bathroom lines into two even partitions.

"Did you just knock his ass out with a slap?" Big Bird asked.

"Yeah," I sighed as I confiscated his gun. "I got into college on a kickboxing sponsorship."

Both Big Bird and a 90s Queen Latifah admired my handiwork with raised brows before nodding towards Maia.

"Girl you better suck his shit good," Queen Latifah said. "That was too smooth."

The lines were suddenly moving fast, and I didn't have time to correct assuming-ass Queen Latifah on the nature of me and Maia's relationship before she got swept towards the stalls.

"I'm sorry about that," I gulped while facing Maia.

"About what? Slapping that lil boy?"

"No, about what that lady said. The di- the sucking part."

"Oh, please," she chuckled. "I'm not offended."

Her eyes followed the lines of my body with quiet approval before she seemingly came back to reality from wherever she was. Then she smiled at me and my whole face tingled. I was blushing like a teenage boy. It was crazy because I was the one who told Luc that we needed to approach Maia together so we didn't accidentally creep her out, and yet at the moment all I wanted to do was ask her if she wanted to smile some more over dinner. I needed to go find my wife immediately.
Well, after I handled the man spread out on the tile.

"Shit, I need to go find somebody for this," I groaned while wrapping the piece in paper towels.
"No need, I already texted Vic," Maia replied while slipping her phone back into costume.
She didn't have pockets on her bottoms like usual, no. Instead her pockets were sewn into the inner lining on her top, which if I was looking, I would say afforded the average peon the perfect view of her buxom cleavage. But I couldn't say for sure because I was staring her in the eyes the entire time. Like a gentleman.

"Jesus Christ, Ermias," she said, meeting my unintentionally intense eye contact. "Are you ok? You look like you saw a ghost."
Correction, I was staring at her like a creep.
"Sorry, I'm good. I'm just shocked that you know Vic. Most people here paid for tickets."
"Yeah, me and his wife Sam go way back. She invites me every year."
"Oh that's cool I didn't know that," I nodded, wondering why Sam never thought to mention her fine ass friend from way back to her supposed favorite cousin.
Sam didn't know it yet, but she was definitely getting socks for Christmas. How dare she?

"How do you know Vic?" Maia asked. "The range?"
I had completely forgotten that Vic was the reason I even knew about the range. He convinced me to sign up so he could get the referral points, and luckily it had been a good fit. Another weird coincidence.
Everything about meeting Maia was starting to feel serendipitous.
"Nah, I know him through Sam too. She's my cousin," I explained. "Believe it or not. I've only been to the range a handful of times."

"Wait, haven't you been a member for like two years?"
"Yeah, unfortunately I have a weird work schedule. So I don't have a lot of daylight hours for free time."
"Tell me about it. But that's why we have midnight sessions."

"I saw you extended them. I signed up for next week's."
"Yeah, I can finally afford the overnight security," she nodded.

Her smile was dusted with a small but healthy amount of pride. She seemed like she was in a good place with the range. I liked the way victory looked on her already. I didn't like to break rules, but I had to make an exception. I'd kick myself if I waited another week, or worse another month, to get to know the woman in front of me. Hopefully Luci would be forgiving tonight with all the free liquor in her system.
"Can I please buy you a drink?" I chuckled.

Maia

This was the greedy bisexual behavior those people were yelling about. I spent two hours laughing and dancing with Luci just to turn around and do the same thing with Ermias. Holding Luci while we rocked felt like holding heaven, but being held by Ermias? I kind of understood the point of straight jackets. His arms around me were so comforting that my mind went white. I didn't even remember us walking back to the bar.

"What are you having?" Ermias asked as he pulled out my chair.
"Mm, just a green tea shot for now," I sighed. "It's getting late." So far I'd been out for five hours and I'd paid for a grand total of one drink. To be fair, my second, third, and fourth had been purchased because my first drink had spilled down my boobs, but the fifth and six were just because. Just because I smiled a little bit after playing the damsel in distress. I wasn't worried about the little boy in the ski mask and denim leggings, but still it was nice of Ermias to defend me.
I didn't get a lot of champions in life.

"I got you," Ermias nodded before flagging down a bartender.
"Say, young man. Let me get a couple drinks from you."
We sat at the bar for 40 minutes sipping Old Fashions while talking about tropical plants, old school shotguns, and pie rankings. Ermias' favorite was apple while mine was classic sweet potato. We had the same runner up of cherry, and apparently he knew about this bakery that had the unofficially official best cherry pie ever. I hated how good of a conversationalist he was because I ain't even feel bad for accidentally losing Luci. I still hoped to see her again after she closed though, and I had a feeling I would. She hadn't given me her number for nothing.

"So, how long have you lived in Atlanta?" I asked, flicking Ermias' antenna.

Ermias was dressed as the Yellow Teletubby and I had to stop myself from giggling every time I looked his way. I don't know why it tickled me so bad. I guess it was the juxtaposition of his benign appearance and his ability to knock niggas out with a single slap.

"How do you know I'm not from Atlanta?" Ermias scoffed, bringing his hand to his chest to feign offence.

"Mhm," I nodded. "Do me a favor real quick. Say baby."

"Come on, Maia. Don't do me like that," he laughed.

Just like I thought. Ermias had a Southern accent, yes. But more specifically, he had a New Orleans accent. It was especially thick on his terms of endearment. I could feel the vibrato of his "baby" in my stomach. That made me wonder what else of his I'd be able to feel in my guts.

"I've been here about three years," he confirmed. "I moved up here for a job with The Atlanta Botanical Garden." "You work for the garden?" I gasped. "That's so fucking cool."

"Yeah, I'm the head landscaper," he nodded.

As I sat there listening to Ermias talk about what an honor it was to design exhibit arrangements and honor his grandparent's legacy, I realized I'd never been impressed with a man before. There was a first time for everything though because I leaned forward onto my hands while we talked, hung up on his every word. Yeah he was handsome, tall, and smart with his dick print visible through multiple layers of velvet, but outside of that he had a nice voice and a very calming presence. He was like the human embodiment of lavender.

"You ok, Maia?" he asked. "Am I being boring? Sorry, I don't get out much. I know I have weird conversation topics."

"No," I assured him, placing my hand over his. "You're not being boring. You're reviving my faith in men."

"Lawd," he chuckled. "Is the dating scene that bad?"

"Yes, absolutely," I nodded. "Fuck piss. The dating pool has brain rotting acid in it. These niggas don't have hobbies, jobs, or clean drawls half the time. And that's just with me meeting people in person. I can't imagine what the apps are like."

"I honestly never got curious enough to download the apps. It just felt like a dignity graveyard."

"It is," I confirmed. "People be tryna to use them to order sex regardless of what your profile says. Nigga this is not BK, you can't have it your way."

"Oh that's a throwback," Ermias chuckled. "You about to have me singing the JG Wentworth jingle in here."

"Do you have a structured settlement?" I giggled.

We did in fact end up singing the JG Wentworth jingle at the bar. Ermias sang as my backup acapella while I belted out the hook with a crazy reverb. Most of the younger folks looked at us like we had a pipe hidden somewhere, but I didn't care. I usually only had loud fun with friends once a year on vacation. This was a nice change of pace.

"Oh look, the band is starting," Erm said while helping me down from the bar counter.

The drums were already beating with a sultry rhythm and the dramatic melodies of a keyboard were right behind it. My ears strained for the sharp zing of a familiar electric guitar but none greeted me.

"Is Luci performing?" I asked as I climbed onto a stool.

"Luci?" he loured. "Lucianna?"

"Yeah. Do you know her?"

"She-"

Ermias' explanation was quickly cut short as the guitar I had been wanting to hear all night zipped quick notes through the air, making my skin tingle with the same electricity as her touch. Luciana looked just as ethereal the second time playing, with her wild kinky curls falling down her back and her excited eyes bouncing through the crowd. She found me and Ermias in the crowd halfway through her third song, and a wide mischievous grin stretched across her plump lips. Time suspended when we locked eyes, and although I knew she was still playing because her fingers were moving, I couldn't hear a thing. All I could hear was my rapid pulse syncing to the rhythm of her hips as she left the stage and parted the crowd. I could feel her body calling mine even before she reached me. I could practically taste the sweetness of her kiss. A kiss I'd been waiting for the entire night.

One as familiar and as fantastical as a dream.

The crowd broke into deafening applause as Luci struck the strings of her guitar for the last time before falling into my lap.

"Everyone give it up for the unforgettable, Lady Luck!" Sam cheered.

A memory suddenly came to the forefront of my mind. Lady Luck, from the band Infallible. No wonder Luci looked so familiar.

"You played for Infallible?" I squealed.

"For a time," she chuckled before looking at Ermias. "I see you've met my husband."

"Your husband!?" I screamed.

Me and Luci were definitely flirting. I was ok with that because when she said she was Poly, I assumed she was already in at least one relationship since she wore a ring. Ermias didn't say shit though. His fingers were bare and he definitely didn't mention being married. Especially not when he was practically drowning in my titties. Did Luci know he was omitting that part? I didn't know, but either way I was ready to fight on her behalf. I took off my shoe and started to launch it at his ass before Luci stopped me.

"Wait! I thought you two were vibing? What happened!?" she shrieked.

"He didn't tell me he was married!" I gritted, feeling familiar pangs of betrayal. "Where's your ring, Ermias?"

I had spent many Halloween nights dealing with lying men and I wouldn't be re-running those episodes. Which is why I was reluctant to loosen my grip on the sole of my boot. I was still holding that mothafucka like a glock, even when Luci tried to calm me with a gentle pat.

"Wait, Maia. I didn't tell you initially because I was waiting on Luci. I promised her we would move as a unit when it came to you. Plus I was about to tell you when Luci got on stage. Also I don't wear my ring out. I've lost three at work," Erm explained sheepishly.

"What do you mean when it comes to me? I just met Luci. When was this conversation?"

Chapter 6

Hear Me Out...

Maia

Another sidecar and thirty minutes later, I was placated. It was the craziest *hear me out* I've entertained to date, but everything made a lot more sense afterwards. Lucianna explained that they had been looking for lucky number three for years now with no luck. Apparently her and Ermias didn't often have the same taste in women. Which is why he went straight home and told Luci when he bumped into me in the hall. If they hadn't met me tonight they would've approached me together and formally asked me out. Erm had even prepared a comparison chart explaining how well we'd all mesh together. It was a crazy amount of effort for someone he'd only met once and I told him that immediately. Yet...

"Come on, Maia. You can't tell me you didn't feel it too. You didn't feel the sparks when we touched in the hall?" Ermias asked.
I remained quiet because otherwise I'd be telling lies, and I didn't feel like lying after 6 drinks. I did feel it and that was the problem. I felt it with both of them. Luci and Erm's presence was a lightning strike to my nervous system. I thought I was ready to date but that was before tonight. I wanted to deal with somebody I enjoyed, not people I adored. I wasn't trying to double my heartbreak. That's exactly what would happen. Hell it'd only been five hours and I was already picturing how'd we spend our one year anniversary.

"We're not going to break your heart, Mai," Luci smiled tentatively.
"You don't know that for sure. Look at you. Those fingers play like they regularly ruin lives."
Luci held up her pointer finger in protest and Ermias quickly lowered it, urging her to be honest. I knew then and there that Erm would be our mediator if I were to entertain them.

He generally seemed stately. Outside of knocking that boy out with a single slap.

"Listen, Luci is a seductress. Yes, that's true," he nodded. "But she's also a lover girl. She knows your birthday is next week and she already picked out a belated birthday gift to give you on our hypothetical first date."

"Luci, did you stalk my Instagram?" I sighed.

"Yes, but not in a creepy way. *More like a "Wow, I can't believe this woman is real,"* way. I was in awe."

"You know you're Lady Luck right?" I chuckled. "I was in awe. I'm still in awe that we're having this conversation. Lady Luck is tryna fuck me."

"Not just fuck," Luci corrected sternly. "I really wanna date you. You have to admit that it kinda feels like we're meant to be."

Everything about our meeting did feel surreal. Like it was something woven together by an experienced quilt maker, every dot and detail a small but necessary piece giving way to the entire story. That in itself scared me. I knew this wasn't something I could control. Which in some ways was exciting.

"I need to go slow. Like straight people slow," I said carefully, trying not to give away too much.

"How slow is that?" Ermias asked.

"Wait two days to call after the first date, slow."

"Can we text?" Luci queried.

"Hm. Maybe if it's limited to memes," I chuckled.

Ermias looked like he was perfectly fine with my limits, but Luci was practically vibrating with anticipation as she bit down on her lower lip. Girl love was different. I knew that from experience. It was vulnerable, and soft, and a little overwhelming at times, but it was almost always worth it.

"It's been a while since I dated anyone," I admitted. "I don't wanna mess this up."

That was when I realized Luci was an empath and effectively a mirror. Her shoulders slumped with mine and her smile was just as cautious as she reached to lace her fingers in mine.

"We'll go slow," she nodded. "I don't wanna mess this up either."

"And I'm here too," Erm chuckled.

"Sorry," me and Luci offered simultaneously.

"Don't be," he said with a dismissing wave. "This is cute. But it's getting late and I need to be up early tomorrow for work. Maia, can we walk you back to your car and get your number to coordinate an actual date?"

"All good, Erm. Luci already has my number. Plus I caught a Muver here. I can walk y'all out though."

"No, Mai-Tai, there's no sense in you paying surge pricing. Let us take you home," Luci offered.

"Are you sure? Haven't you both been drinking?"

"I don't really get drunk," Erm shrugged. "I'm too big. It takes four drinks for me to even get buzzed. So I'll happily be your designated driver."

I barely fought back the urge to grin. Braving Atlanta traffic after a party for a woman you weren't technically dating yet was modern day chivalry. Some of my training from the Dial-Up Internet era screamed at me to remember stranger danger, but I wasn't honestly concerned. Sam pulled me aside after she watched me dancing with Luci and confirmed Luci was good people. Vic let me know I was in good hands as long as I was with Ermias.

Plus my coochie had a heartbeat and she hardly ever steered me wrong. Her intuition rivaled the late great, Octavia Butler's.

"Ok," I nodded. "I can still give you a little gas money."

They both looked disgusted, but it was the right thing to do. I at least needed to offer, even if it made Luci clutch her pearls.

"Follow Luci and take yo pretty behind to the car," Ermias laughed with a dismissive head shake.

Chapter 7

Girls Just Wanna Have

...

Ermias

Our wedding day remained vivid in my memories even six years later. I remembered how bright the sun shone despite the fact that we got married in mid February. I remembered the softly cascading piano notes announcing Luci's arrival. And I really remembered how tight my pants and tie felt the second I saw her at the end of the aisle, her wild curls only slightly tamed, but her rum and coke eyes just as mischievous. I remembered holding her close at the end of the night and wholly thinking that she'd be the only one for me. How could I ever want more than this? I couldn't.

Yet now, Maia was proving that statement a lie. I wanted her the way bees wanted balloon flowers. Especially while seeing her and Luci together, spread out across the black leather upholstery of the back seat, hands and legs tangled in a sea of rich, moisturized, complimentary brown. They were busy kissing so they didn't see me staring like a starving lion in the rearview mirror, and I was too hypnotized by their soft touching, nipping, and giggling to interrupt.

They started slow, but I soon noticed enticing flashes of skin and restless, hungry touches. Two sets of hands teased thighs, and cupped breasts, and held hips as the two of them synced to a comfortable rhythm in the limited space. I probably would've let them be and explore in any other circumstance, but then I heard them moan. Maia's voice was a gentle crescendo while Luci sounded like the trouble she was. She was raspy, yet calm as Maia took one of her nipples into her mouth. I was uncomfortably hard from their sounds alone, but then I saw the dark purple of Maia's lipstick staining Luci's chest.

"Ladies, you have two options," I barked, trying to capture their attention. "If you'd like to continue, we can go back home to me and Luci's, or we can stop here for the night if you'll have us, Maia. But either way, we need to be out of this car in the next 26 and a half minutes."

"And what's gonna happen if we don't?" Luci teased from her spot on Maia's chest.

"If you can't settle on a place then I'll pick one. Which will likely be on the hood of the truck. Or we can open the trunk, let down the seats, and put on a show."

"Is that a trick or a treat?" Maia asked.

"Both," I confirmed with a chuckle.

Maia's house suited her. It was moody but still bright in some spots, with lush, green plants all around and citrus-colored artwork hanging from the walls. The hardwood was dark and spotless, and I could see our candlelit reflections in it. Which made it easy to enjoy the view of the ladies when I took my shoes off. I watched in awe as Maia unzipped Luci's skirt in one quick, eloquent movement only for Luci to step out of it with the same gracefulness. Maia's hands which were once supporting Luci as she stripped, then came to Luci's hips effortlessly. Women had a thousand times more finesse than men.

They were nearly naked in an instant and I was tripping over the legs of my suit to at least meet them halfway. I didn't have plans to interrupt them because I knew that women needed a long warming period, but I wanted to be available when they needed me. If I was needed at all. Luci and Maia stood in the center of the living room, drawing each other's breath with hungry kisses, bodies pressed tight, grinding in perfect sync through the thin barriers of their panties. It was dizzying watching their curves race against each other. Dizzying enough to numb the shock that Luciana was even wearing panties.

When their heaving became too much, Maia voluntarily freed her breasts from the tight confines of her bra, allowing her generous mounds to spill free. Me and Luci's gaze dipped down to her dinner plate areolas, each topped with a cacao nib of a nipple that was drawn hard and tight.

"You have really pretty titties," Luci sighed while lifting one of Maia's boobs closer to her watering mouth.

"No you," Maia moaned as Luci's lips closed around the stiff

peaks.
Maia's hands slipped down and around Luci's ass to massage her pussy while she simultaneously arched her back, allowing Luci all the access she could ever want.

My dick became painfully hard watching the efficient degenerates in front of me. Although I swore I wouldn't interrupt, I had to take my underwear off. My dick bobbed against my belly as I rolled my waistband down, and a single sticky drop of precum fell from my tip onto the hardwood. The amount was too insignificant to make a sound, and yet when I looked back up to see what the girls were doing, their eyes were trained on me.

"Do we make you horny, Ermias?" Luci teased while massaging Maia's nipples. "Do you like watching Maia play with my pussy?"
Maia grinned as she spun Luci around to face me, pressing Luci's back against her front. She used her bent knee to spread Luci's legs open against her own, and then two fingers to part her puffy lips. I swallowed a knot while watching Luci's wetness glide down her brown skin, leaving a slick trail in its wake, and I nearly cried watching Maia's pointer and middle finger sink into my wife.

Luci's head fell back into the pillowy abyss of Maia's breasts as Maia pumped her fingers in and out of my favorite sticky, fat cat. Then the two of them occupied their free hands with each other's needy nipples. My dick was just weeping. I wrapped my hand around the base of my shaft and squeezed, attempting to feel something else besides undeniable need, and the girls lit up.
Nasty lil things.
I could tell they wanted to watch me jack it, but I wouldn't give them the satisfaction so soon.

"Luci's so wet and sticky, Ermias," Maia cooed with a pout. "Come taste her."
I shook my head no, barely resisting the temptation to crawl over on my hands and knees and rub my face in their mess.
And what a glorious mess it was. Silky brown thighs pressed together with a mix of their wetness, kiss-swollen mouths slick with drool, and lipstick marked breasts that swayed and bounced with each seductive movement. It was a beautiful thing that I just wanted to watch and witness. I was not trying to potentially disappoint two women at once. I was ready to buss right then and I hadn't even touched them.

"We make him nervous, Mai," Lucianna moaned. "He's scared."

"Yes, cause I'm smart," I sneered back. "You two ain't nothing but trouble."

"Who, us?" they pouted in tandem.

Great. Now I was getting suckered double-time. More always sounds good in theory. A million dollar house sounds better than a hundred thousand dollar one until you get the tax bill. That was where I was now. Reaping the consequences of living large.

Yet I couldn't really find any regret in my heart as I looked between the two breathtaking women standing in front of me. They were going to run me ragged tonight. That was a fact I knew well. I also knew that they would be ganging up on me for the foreseeable future. If I had more blood flow to my brain I probably would've been concerned, but all I could show concern for right then was how we'd all fit on Maia's bed when I finally fucked them.

"Come here," I growled. "Both of you."

Luci

We were in trouble. We talked a good game up until Erm bit back. People were constantly reminded not to poke the bear but me and Maia decided to throw rocks at ours.

Ours.

That sounded so right and it felt even better. Especially because we were collectively getting our shit rocked by a nasty man coming down off of brown liquor. Ermias had incredible dexterity from years of horticulture work, and he was flexing his skills by playing with me and Maia's pussy in tandem. Our hands were intertwined between us, shaking so hard that they were practically vibrating as we rode out the aftershocks of our latest orgasms.

"What's wrong?" he chuckled while rubbing our clits. "Ain't this what you wanted?"

I knew what I was signing up for, but Maia, that poor baby was unprepared. She squeezed my hand as hard as she could while she mounted her third release in ten minutes. I knew she was sensitive and overstimulated because her legs shook like a set of maracas. Yet I was of no help because I was also circling the drain.

"I'm s-s-orry," I whined.

I wasn't, and Erm knew that. Yet he grinned in response to my faux apology, treating it more like a trophy than real progress. His lips met Maia's first for a tender, tentative kiss, and then mine for something rougher and more volatile. I came first and Maia followed shortly behind me, making easy work of

wetting up our makeshift floor palette. Satisfied with his work, Ermias slowly pulled his thick fingers from us and brought them to his mouth. Mine first, and then Maia's.
"Mmm, Luci you gotta try this," he groaned while sucking his middle finger clean. "She's so sweet."

Maia's chest rose and fell with each labored breath as she came back down from post orgasmic bliss, and I was perfectly content to watch her. My eyes fell low and I snuggled in close, allowing myself to get comfortable. Right until Ermias pinched our clits.
"What the fuck, Erm?" Maia loured.
"Yeah, what the fuck?" I parroted.
"The fuck is you thinking I was going to allow y'all a moment of peace after you two spent the last hour trying my sanity."
"We were just playing," Maia pouted, ejecting her bottom lip.
"Play with each other, not with me," Erm grinned. "Speaking of playing with each other, Maia, you should let Luci taste you."

Suddenly my prior drowsiness had dissipated. My senses all came back online at once, and I realized I was laying against a woman. A soft, naked, warm woman whose pussy smelled like honey. I gave Maia a pleading look and she smiled softly in return. A silent, *go ahead.* I was careful as I slid down the length of her body and settled in between her legs. I even fought the urge to suck on her gorgeous midnight nipples again. Although just barely.

I looked over my shoulder to spot Ermias. Who was stationed behind us watching with his head in his hands, wearing a look of pure adoration as I kissed up Maia's thighs. It was the same look he gave me, his wife of five years.
I understood it though. Maia was easy to adore. Kind, smart, and hilarious. All while being mind- numbingly beautiful. So beautiful that I wanted pictures of her hanging in every room of the house. I knew we had only just met but I was already beginning to fall in love.

"Lucianna," Maia whimpered. "Please, baby girl."
Her voice broke me from my delusional visions of our future, then I met her eyes. Her pupils were so big they almost appeared black. Little voids that you could easily lose your soul in. Portals to the unknown.

The skin on my back prickled with the presence of magic as I dipped my head to place a kiss on her lower lips, and it spread across my entire body with Maia's bellowing moan. Ermias was right, she was sweet. Sweet like a sticky mango on a hot summer's day. Ever the glutton, I sucked and licked her just like the aforementioned fruit as her fingers twined around my curls. She was incredibly responsive, squeezing around my fingers while I worked them in and out of her tight pussy. I felt a brief pang of jealousy, mostly because Erm would be able to appreciate her tightness more than I ever could. The world was too kind to men.

"Sorry, Luci," Ermias groaned as he parted my legs to tease his tip against my sex.
I knew he was watching, but I didn't give him and his view much thought since I was laid up like a snipper eating the box. However, if the tip of his dick was any indication of the rest of his length, he was rigid and throbbing. We hadn't touched him besides a few kisses, but apparently we didn't need to. Watching us was plenty inspiring. "You're making me lose focus," I whined as he teased me.
"Is this better?" he chuckled while finally stretching me open.
"Much," I hissed.

My hips rolled forward on their own volition, assisting my arch, and allowing me to take him with ease. I hadn't realized how wet I was until he slipped inside of me. Yet it made sense. How could I not be considering the perfect pretty princess I had in front of me? Let alone the beefcake we had torturing us. The one that was currently digging me out while he tapped my clit along to the rhythm of Masego's saxophone.
"Bounce that ass against that fat dick, baby," Maia cooed. "Fuck him back."

Her gentle encouragement worked in unity with Erm's deep, rhythmic moans to overwhelm me. Before long I was cumming completely out of rhythm with my mouth full of hot pussy. Maia used her grip on my hands to bounce me back when I could no longer remember how to work my legs. Ermias' grip on my hips was just barely holding me up after each driven thrust. I was just lucid enough to realize that I was shaking from the force of another orgasm. "Fuck," I cried out before letting my teeth sink into my lower lip.
We shifted at my outcry, causing my nipples to scrape against the cotton edging of the blanket beneath me, working my already spent nerves even further, and I fell onto Maia's belly with an exasperated groan.

I expected to be human jello after a nut like that, but somehow I had the strength to sit up.
And when I saw everything I had in front of me, I used it to locate Maia's nipples.
She let me fill my mouth uninterrupted for a few minutes before she pulled me up for a kiss.
Soft then hungry, slow, and intentional. Her tongue teased

mine, pulling it along the edges of the space where our lips met. I knew she was several drinks deep but she still tasted faintly of mint, clean and addicting. Our hips began to roll along to the pace set by our kissing, and soon we were at it again. Our clits were pressed together, thumping and jumping with each soft nip and greedy caress. Ermias once again proved how perceptive he was by adding his fingers to the mix at just the right time by giving us something to squeeze as we rode out another wave.

This one didn't leave us breathless, instead we were both wide-eyed and voracious. Ready for whatever came next.
"Luci, can I fuck your husband?" Maia asked softly while stroking my back.
She didn't have to ask, but the fact that she did, and so carefully at that made me like her even more. I really hoped she didn't try to ghost us after this because I had every intention to keep her. I passed Ermias a look silently expressing just that and he didn't protest. He just grinned and shook his head. I guess he was already setting up our first, second, and third date in his head. Knowing and having dated him before, I knew each one of them would be over the top and delightful.

"Ermias, do you wanna fuck Maia?" I asked, interrupting his train of thought. "I think you should. She's sooo tight and wet."
I proved my point by pushing my middle finger back inside her slowly. She rocked against my hand, letting out a satisfying moan as I prepared her for something a little bit more substantial. I was still jealous that I didn't have a dick to put in her, but I could live vicariously through Erm.

"You're so pretty," I cooed while meeting her for a kiss. "And this pussy is so good."
"I'll be the judge of that," Erm said, adding his finger with mine.
Lust slowly bled back into his gaze. The type of primal lust that reminded me that humans were animals too. If I wasn't so turned on I might have been scared for Maia.

"We're both clean, I promise," he whispered to Maia. "But do you have condoms? I wanna make sure you're comfortable until we can prove it."
We had full STD panels scheduled for next week in anticipation of our potential date with Maia, but in a wild turn of events, we ended up between her legs before either one of those things could happen. Ermias was right, we were clean, but we hadn't been tested since our last partner, 2 years ago.

"I got some," Maia nodded while pointing toward her room. "In the bottom left drawer under the socks."

Ermias acknowledged the newly given information with a gentle hum, however he was still curling his fingers around inside her, trapped in a pussy daze. "I got it," I offered. "You can keep playing."
Maia gave me a soft peck for my volunteer work before I wandered into her room to locate the rubbers. I was supposed to be thinking about hot, nasty sex, but the fuzzy feeling in my chest grew when I saw how she filled her space.

The walls were painted a rich burgundy, a moody color that was still vibrant enough to compliment the sensuality of the art and sculptures she'd chosen. There was a large bookshelf in one corner filled to the brim with paperbacks stacked haphazardly in front of the hardcovers, and the bottom of the shelf was dedicated to vintage records with covers that showed their age and their modern relevance. Ermias probably would've rifled through a few and eventually settled on the Why Do Fools Fall In Love Vinyl. However, I was most interested in her bed and the pictures surrounding it.

There were dozens of pictures of her friends and family on the wall directly opposite from where her pillow nest lay. It was both sweet and anxiety-inducing, because I could tell from the happy shots that she was well loved, and the last thing I wanted to do was live up to the sometimes toxic, girl-love stereotype and break her heart. Especially since that had been her main hesitation just hours earlier.

"Luci, are you ok, hun?" Maia called breathlessly. "We miss you."
I smiled, hearing her call me hun. It was just a small thing but that, combined with her soft tone helped to abate the rest of my fears.
I didn't want to break her heart so I simply wouldn't. Instead I'd just break her back.
No correction, *we'd* break her back.
Together.

I got giddy while imagining her first time with Ermias, although it was just minutes away, and I dug through her bottom drawer like a mad woman. I spotted the gold-backed wrappers once I cleared away the impressive amount of mated socks. A whole bankroll band of them. At least I knew she was used to safe sex. However, there was something else in there too that really had my attention.

Chapter 8

Sticky Situation

Maia

"Ok, ready," Luci announced.
I looked up from my spot underneath Ermias to spot Lucinanna standing proud in the doorway, wearing nothing but her tattoos, a borrowed pair of fuzzy socks, and a strap sporting a baby-pink corn cob monster. My favorite corn cob monster.
"I see you've gotten comfy," I laughed.
"A lil bit," she nodded. "My feet were cold."
"I should've warned you that she was a clothing thief," Ermias chuckled.

I never considered myself to be anything other than a femme, but seeing Luci wear my clothes filled me with a strange amount of joy and pride. I wondered if that was how dudes felt when they saw their girlfriends in their hoodies for their first time.
Girlfriend. Was Luci my girlfriend?

No, it was too soon. But I damn sure wanted her to be. Amazing pussy and head game aside, she was the type of woman I could see myself growing old with. You know, building a life, having kids, and becoming two bickering old ladies who went to rummage sales on the weekend and gossiped with their mostly disinterested husband as he pruned back plants.
Yeah, I could see that.

"Although I highly doubt you'll be dissatisfied with Erm's services, I did want to make myself available should you need me," she explained while throwing the cob in a circle.
"How considerate of you," I teased with a slight pout. "Now can you please come give me a kiss? I'm trying to decide which one of y'all is better at it."
"I am," she and Erm declared simultaneously.

"Ope," I squeaked while looking between them.
The divas were competing.

Ermias looked the most appalled, which surprised me because his dick was still actively thumping against my stomach, but I guess he had enough brain power to manage both of his emotions.
"Lucianna," he chuckled. "Now I ain't tryna take away your accomplishments, but come on, baby. I can tie a thong in a knot."
"I am," Luci shrugged matter of factly. "Your little party trick doesn't make you the better kisser, it just makes you more freaked out. Kissing is about how you make the kissee feel."
"Well, then I still win because I make your heart flutter," Ermias tutted, trying to be sweet.
"Yeah, you do," Luci conceded. "But I made you nut in your pants."
"She's got you there," I nodded from my spot underneath his bicep.

Ermias was telling me about that when Luci was off procuring rubbers. Apparently he made the mistake of taking her dancing on their second date. He was naive and figured he could handle it. But while the ass shaking didn't do him, her hungry, demanding kisses did.
"I have better dick game," he harrumphed.
"You better!" I said tickling his side. "Yours is attached."
"Exactly! Tell him Mai-Tai."
"Here y'all go with that gang up shit," Ermias playfully huffed.
"Gang bang shit?" I grinned.
"Train gang?" Luci laughed.

Me and Luci continued to exchange puns as Ermias moved about the room, collecting pillows as he did. I was about to tease him for building a nest, but when I looked over to see what he was doing, I realized he had used the cushions to rig up two queening chairs.
"Did I mention I was almost a structural engineer?" Ermias grinned in response to my shocked expression.
"I was almost a teacher," I replied. "I figured I could rock a thrifted cardigan and teach the youth. But I ended up changing my mind because I couldn't deal with the parents."
"Girl, my best friend retired from teaching because of the parents. Somebody's mama tried to fight her," Luci responded.
"What!?" I gasped, reeling to hear more.

Erm cleared his throat with a long chuckle.
"Luci, that is a brunch story. And while I don't mean to be crass or dismissive, it's not a story I'm in the mood to hear. I want somebody sitting on my dick and somebody else on my

beard. Now."
Ermias stroked his length hard and slow while I sat with Luci
in my arms. His one eyed monster was glistening with a drop
of thick, clear, precum. His dick was a bit darker than the
rest of him, the perfect shade of complimentary ebony which
highlighted the left-leaning curve of his elephant trunk. I
always had a thing for big, beefy men and the one in front
of me was perfect. From his moisturized chestnut skin, to his
bright hazel eyes, and his plush, two-toned, bow-shaped lips.
Lips that were curled into a frown because me and Luci hadn't
moved a muscle.
"Ladies," he barked menacingly, provoking us into action.

We scrambled off the floor and headed in different directions.
I headed south to head up the angry pole waving in my direc-
tion, and Luci headed north wet up his beard.
She reluctantly abandoned her strap while I sat on Ermias's
thighs, curiously stroking his length. He was just as responsive
as Lucianna under my touch. Hissing, cussing, and bucking
against my hand. More of that tempting pre-cum beaded on
his tip and I started to bend forward and taste some, but Luci
beat me to it. With her ass shaking over Erm's forehead, she
pursed her lips around the tip of him. Her slow bob eventually
led her to where my hand was still settled, and we began
working in tandem with her next movement.

"You look so gorgeous when you suck dick," I purred before
pushing Luci's hair from her eyes.
Her swollen, round, rosy lips, her watery brownie-colored
eyes, and her flushed face only added to her natural beauty.
Seeing her unbound and unguarded made my heart flip, especially when she grinned at me. I left my position to meet
her lips, all while keeping Erm's pulsing length between us.
Of course he responded in kind by gripping the cushions half
to death. Yet me and Luci could barely contain our delighted
giggles as Erm writhed underneath our coordinated torture.

If I ever bothered to make a checklist for what I wanted in
a male partner, Ermias would hit every single one. He was
gentle, patient, kind, and intelligent. He was also tall and
muscular, but still soft enough to find comforting on a cold
night, and he had a fat, wide dick with enough stamina not to
buss while two fine ass women had their way with him. All of
that was very good, but then he had to go and moan.

It was loud, smooth, and reverberating. With his first groan
flowing into his second like an Acapella hymn. The shock-
waves from the depth of his voice vibrated against my pussy,
encouraging my hand to leave the base of his shaft and travel
to my needy clit.

Soon, the three of our voices harmonized from the delightful pleasure of each other, and while Ermias could seemingly handle whatever the world threw at him, that was his limit. He sat up, disrupting us both, snatched a strip of condoms off the couch, sheathed himself, and then pulled me and Luci exactly where we wanted us. First I was pulled back into his lap with my wobbly knees the only difference between the threat of impalement, while Luci was repositioned onto his shoulders. "Sit down, both of you," he demanded.

I raised up while Luci scooched back. She had just enough leverage remaining to position Ermias' tip at my entrance, and on the count of three, we slowly lowered ourselves onto our targets. Ermias took control of our pace after his initial breach. With his hands holding my hips tight, he was intentionally slow, only feeding me an inch with each shallow stroke. Every inch ruined me.

By the fifth, the satisfying feeling of fullness was so great that a tear rolled down my cheek. I never had someone fit inside me so right. Every frustrated, insatiable, confused moment I had over the last month had been righted instantly. I wasn't even mad about my ex anymore. I was just grateful for everything that happened so that I could share that moment with them. I guess the tears had Luci concerned at first, but when she reached for me and I melted into her arms, she understood that I was just overwhelmed.

"I know, mamas," she cooed while pecking me. "He's a little too good at plumbing pipes sometimes."
"So good," I nodded while nuzzling her chest. "These fucking veins. Oh my God, Ermias."
The slight burn of the first stretch had faded, and left in its place was all the tingly pleasure that came with being filled to the max while watching one of the most beautiful women you'd ever seen tremble and convulse in front of you. My body heated as I met Luci for another kiss, and as her hands came to cup my jaw and my swaying breasts, I was transported back into my dream.

Rough and soft, gentle, and greedy. Two opposing forces who worked in tandem to unravel me. Luci stole the air right out of my lungs while Ermias pumped me full. His unyielding stiffness coupled with Luci's comforting softness couldn't be anything other than a sin. The memories of my dreams were vivid and blurred with my reality. The lines are so blurred that I held my breath, waiting to feel the signature hot-cold that was inflicted on me all the times before. Instead all I got was searing heat as Luci pulled my nipple into her mouth and sent me and Ermias tumbling over the edge together.

"I almost had it," he grumbled as Luci rose. "The squirting surprised me."

I glanced down to spot his glistening lap beneath our point of union. Erm was still semi hard. Hard enough to make me stretch around him like a T-shirt two sizes too small. He was a lot like Angel, and while I realized I should've been sore and exhausted, the sight of us made me wanna go again.

"I know that look," he said with a disappointed sigh. "Give me ten minutes and let me drink some water."

"I can make it five if you got some honey," Luci offered.

"Yes!" I nodded enthusiastically before breaking me and Erm's seal.

Then the mess underneath us worsened. Wetness smeared everywhere. I knew I would need a hot bath but I doubted any amount of heat and soap would be able to remove the stains from the blanket we were on.

"I'll clean that up in a sec," I grimaced.

I left Luci and Ermias to their own devices in the kitchen while I handled the puddle. While I soaked up the sopping wet mess and relished the sound of their laughter, a thought passed through my mind. One that reminded me how much I usually hated new people lingering in my personal space. In fact Luci and Ermias were the first party pick-ups that I hadn't suggested a cheap hotel meetup to in years. When I thought about why I discovered that I didn't fear for my safety or boundaries with them. They reminded me of the home I found in my group, just closer in proximity.

Speaking of reminders...

"Mai," Luci purred while rubbing my back. "Erm's almost done recovering, but there's something I wanna try."

The strap was back, and she had a small bowl of honey in one hand and a thermos mug of ice chips in the other. The honey had a looser consistency when she tipped the bowl forward to let me see it.

"It's a little warm, but I promise I won't burn you," she whispered.

"Ok," I nodded. "I trust you."

For a brief, yet uncomfortable, second, I once again thought of my granny and what she would say if she saw me being so trusting. She'd probably ask if I met Luci's mama and if I ran a background check. You know, the responsible thing. Unfortunately, remembering to pop on a condom before I broke my six month abstinence streak was as responsible as I was going to get tonight.

"Where do you want me?" I asked as Luci crept closer.
"Wherever you're comfortable," she whispered.
I settled against the middle of the couch without much fuss. My couch was another thing that made me unsure if I should be trusted with adult money. I bought it specifically for the ease of fucking it provided.
"Let me know if it's too hot," Luci cooed. "Matter of fact, what's your safe word, mamas?"
"Sidecar," I smiled while kissing her grinning face.

All night I had been trying to figure out our preferences and it finally clicked when Luci had me squeeze my titties together so she could drizzle hot honey on my areolas. Ermias was undeniably a dom, and not just any dom, but a pleasure dom. I could both take charge and finger fuck Lucianna in front of her salivating husband, and get pounded like a good girl without much fuss. Switches were tricky. I could admit that. Yet, Luci was the trickiest of us all. She was a bratty switch. She had no limits and no reservations. She was just chaotic energy, raw sex appeal, and intriguing mystery. Fitting for a reformed rockstar.

She brought her thumbs to my nipples to smear the golden liquid across my entire breast, and her enjoyment of the way my breath caught in my throat made obvious in her pleased smirk. It was warm, borderline hot, and it felt oddly slick instead of expectedly sticky. Just like my pussy.
"You look so wet and gooey," she grinned. "So messy."
"It's so messy, baby," I nodded. "But who's gonna clean it up?"

Suddenly Luci looked beyond words. Instead her head dipped down to my cleavage so she could drag her tongue over the tops of my tits. Watching her clean me sent my already fragile string of sanity into orbit. She was carefully working her way from the outside in, determined to kick up every last sweet, golden drop.

I thought that this was the peak of our performance. How could anything get any better than the soothing warmth of

Lucianna when she spread honey all over me? The answer was simple:
It couldn't.
Or at least I believed that before she slipped a cube of ice under her tongue and then rolled it across my nipples.

I arched off the couch to allow my toes to fully curl into the carpet. My back was the world's most perfect bell curve as Lucianna teased my sensitive nerves with her frigid kisses. A sobbing shudder wracked my body and I began to shatter, remembering the prophesized juxtaposition relayed to me in my dreams. It felt sinfully right but I couldn't tell if Lucianna was a blessing or a curse.

"Luci, please," I whined. "I can't take it."
"You're doing so good for me, mamas," she sighed while switching nipples. "So good."
I felt the tip of the cob tease my entrance and I slowly sank down the length of it, meeting Luci's hips with my own.
"Fuck," I whimpered as she teased me with shallow strokes.

My mouth was rewarded with honey-sweet kisses for the tortured moan that slipped out of me and I was once-again reminded of the prowess of women. Lucianna knew exactly what to do at any given time. If I sped up, she met my measures with an ass-rippling force. If I slowed down then she helped me catch my breath with soft pecks and needy squeezes. Then when Ermias returned from his recovery break she pulled him down to join us, inviting his mouth to mine, and pushing onto him while pulling out of me.

We moved in sync like the pistons of an engine, everyone's hips moving up or down to the same rhythm, the same beat. I never felt prouder to be one of those greedy bisexuals the world talked about so much as I stole a taste of Luci's pussy from Ermias' lips, and then a sweet dose of honey from his wife's. My left hand wrapped around Erm's forearm while my right came around to grip a handful of Luci's ass. I could feel Ermias' balls against my ass as he pounded into Luci and she pounded into me. I was carried up and down on the wave of overwhelmed pleasure until I heard the sweet harmonizing of both of their voices, prompting me to sink into the swirling black hole of my orgasm. Then the two of them sank with me, all of us becoming puddles after such a cataclysmic finish. I brought my hand to Luci's back and held her tighter as she shuddered, hoping to give her some of the same warmth she gave me moments earlier.

"I hope you know," she sighed. "I be trying to beat the toxic woman-love allegations, but I'm thinking about popping up

here if you try to ghost me."
"Luci, that's not how you ask people to be your girlfriend,"
Erm chided.
I barely held in my laugh as Luci's eyes rolled around in her
head. She was such a cute ass brat and I couldn't help the
way my heart fluttered when I pecked her. Even though she
threatened my peace moments ago.
"Luci, you don't have to stalk me to get me to be your girlfriend," I whispered while nuzzling her. "Just ask me nicely."
"Let us take you to dinner first before I ask," she cooed while
caressing me back. "I know we just fucked and all, but Chivalry
is not dead."

"Ermias was right," I grinned while pecking her. "You're such
a lover girl."
"Speaking of being right," Erm groaned while disrupting our
post-sex huddle.

He slowly rose to a sitting position behind Luci, hung his
head in shame, and then stood. We both watched him with
concerned expressions as he practically limped over to the
pile that contained his pants, bent forward, and pulled out his
wallet. He then passed Luci a crisp $20 bill to her absolute
delight, as her victorious cackle filling the room.
"Don't be so smug," Ermias sighed as Luci did a little dance.
"I take it you lost a bet?" I giggled.
"Big time," he nodded.

I had been fucked too thoroughly to inquire further about the
details of their bet, but luckily Luci volunteered that information.
"Erm showed me your picture when you bumped into each
other at the range, and I bet him $20 you had some of the best
pussy ever," Luci explained.
"Oh."

I was flattered, and a little turned on, but my body immediately
protested the thought of more. My muscles burned from the
intensity of our midnight menage a trois. It took me almost a
full minute just to get off the floor. I needed a soak, but that
would have to wait until the morning because otherwise I'd
probably drown in the tub. I was so tired I hardly wanted to
walk the fifteen feet to my bed. I needed sleep.

"I promise I'm not trying to weird you out," Ermias said. "But
would you mind if we spent the night? I know that was a lot
and I wanna take care of you."
Again, I thought about what Granny would say. She'd probably
tell me to say no, remind me that they were strangers who
could potentially rob me blind while I slept peacefully, and

yet even with that possibility I nodded my sleepy little head to say yes. Then I yelped as I was swept off my feet into Erm's arms before Luci hopped on his back. We were easily 400 extra pounds and yet he was unaffected. His steps were only slowed slightly.

"Want me to take your wig off for you?" Luci asked while rubbing my scalp. "I keep bond dissolver in my purse."
"What don't you have in that purse?" I giggled.
"The only thing she doesn't carry in that thing is money," Ermias sighed while laying us on my bed.
"Yeah cause that's what you're for," Luci giggled.

I got nervous for a minute after hearing Lucianna's unintended reminder that they were an established couple. We worked together well sexually, but that didn't always translate romantically. I wondered how our relationship would work. How long would I feel like an outsider?
"You don't gotta keep money in your purse either, Mai," Luci chuckled while kissing my cheek. "Big daddy got it for the both of us."

Something told me I wouldn't feel that way for long. Especially when Luci wrapped her arms around my waist and pulled me closer. We snuggled under the comforter with our legs intertwined and our foreheads pressed together. We looked like a pair of cats, but I didn't care because it was the perfect position for a long night's rest.

Well until Erm came back with hot wash cloths and as promised by Luci, bond dissolver.
"Can I get anybody a snack? I think there's a couple of corner stores still open," he offered while wiping me clean.
"No, I'm fine. You, Luc?"
"All good," she replied with a pitchy yawn.
"Ok, but I need you both to finish a couple ounces of water," he conceded.

Despite Luci being just as boneless as I was, she gently removed my hot-ass wig, taking great care with my edges and my nape. Ermias chuckled as we both groaned in relief, and after he made sure everyone was clean, comfortable, hydrated, and wigless, he slipped into bed with a soft thud. At first he stayed off to the side, content to let me and Luci have our moment, but eventually we successfully convinced him to lay in the middle while we both got a side of his chest.

"He's warm," I yawned.
"I know," Luci nodded. "It's the best. Especially in the winter."
"Is it too soon to start planning matching holiday pajamas?"

Erm asked.

"Nope," I sighed. "I already have some saved in my cart. I really like-"

Me and Luci had a preference for plaids while Ermias liked the festive prints. The pajamas were a battle he'd lost, but that was fine because he ultimately won the right to plan our next three dates. I was usually the planner in my relationships but it was nice to free up that brain power. Instead I used it to discuss pretty dresses with Luci. Eventually our conversations slowed to a slur of soft hums peppered with intermittent snoring. I think I was the first to slip into slumber because the last thing I could recall was Luci playing in my loosened braids before whispering,

"Good night, dream girl. You're the best thing I've ever manifested."

Chapter 9

Destiny's Interlude

Dream girl.
My dreams were warm and inviting, like a poolside recliner on a temperate morning. They were full of soft giggling, blurred memories of midnight in hazy veils of seductive black and passionate red, and visions of unrealized futures between us. Visions of cozy breakfasts, midnight serenades, and midday kisses. Visions of vacations, good scotch, vintage rings, and then...
The peach was back.

This time however, it was clutched in Luci's fingers instead of my own, and she offered it to me outright with a smile that could light up a metropolis. Maybe even the entire world if I was selfless enough to share it. Unfortunately Ermias was the only other person who I felt was worthy of such a blessing. We collided on either side of the peach and he caught us with a beat of booming laughter as we fell into each other, my hands on Luci's back and her hands around my waist, both of us completely ignorant of the tripping hazards around us. He gave us a chastising look, silently begging us to be careful. Even though the semi-conscious part of me knew it hadn't happened in real life yet, this part of me, the dreamer, she knew that in that moment I loved them with all my heart. It was a love so great that it stayed with me when a certain rich, silky voice welcomed me back to reality.

"Good morning," Ermias cooed while rubbing both of our backs.
I opened my eyes to a late, golden morning with Luci's hands still threaded through my hair and the scent of a hearty, spice-heavy breakfast. The blanket creased around me as Luci also started to wake, and her wild hair tickled my lower lip.
"Good morning," I croaked, feeling the consequences of my actions.

"Hungover?" he sighed.
"A little."

I stretched from my arms down to the tips of my toes and my body groaned in protest.
"Sore too."
"Well, you need to soak to ease the soreness, but I can help with the hungover part a little. I made turnovers, eggs, bacon, and potatoes."
"I didn't know I had half of those things," I confessed while blinking the sleep out of my eyes.
"You didn't," he chuckled. "I ordered some stuff."
"Wait," me and Luci exclaimed simultaneously. "Didn't you have work today?"

After working through the shock of me and Luci's tandem talking, Ermias shook his head and grinned.
"Meh, it's Saturday. They're just doing some sowing for spring. They can manage without me. Besides, I thought I should be here when you both woke up."
My heart fluttered when I met his starry-eyed gaze. I didn't know what reason I expected to hear, yet I knew it wasn't that. Most men would happily dip out the morning after being sucked and fucked within an inch of their life. Luci was clearly happy but it was nice to see that Ermias would prioritize spending time with us. It was a reminder that he wasn't like most men.

His hands came to cup the sides of our faces before he leaned in to give us two quick pecks each.
"Freshen up and come eat," he said, leaving our sides. "I hope you don't mind, Maia, but I set the table."
"Fine by me," I whispered. I knew dream me was in love for inexplicable reasons, but current me could definitely get used to this. Every single part of it.

Luci

Not even Ermias' hatch chilli eggs and rosemary potatoes could cure The Great Halloween Hangover of 25'. Me and Maia were both famished so we cleared our plates and then some, but when it was time to get dressed and neither one of us could bear to face the vanity lights of the bathroom sink, I knew we needed to bring in something heavy duty.
We needed the tea.

"Ermias, have you had this tea before?" Maia asked as we passed the Cap't Loui.
Erm's truck was tinted but both of us still needed sunglasses to tame the headache lurking in the afternoon sun. We'd already

met our max dose of pain relievers, and yet Maia remained a skeptic of tea power.

"I have," Erm nodded.

"And what did it taste like?"

"Kinda citrusy," he admitted. "Her flu tea tastes like Robitussin though."

"Stop snitching!" I fussed. "Now she's not gonna wanna drink it when the time comes."

"Luci, are you trying to take care of me when I'm sick?" Maia giggled.

"Baby, I'm tryna take care of you always," I grinned. "In sickness and in health."

"Speaking of health," Ermias sighed as we turned onto our street. "Please feel free to soak your bones. Luci commissioned a custom tub through some of her old industry connects."

"I don't know how I keep forgetting Luci's famous," Maia murmured.

"Ex-famous," I corrected. "I live a quaint, quiet, Southern Belle life now."

"You have a girlfriend and a husband," Maia argued. "That's far from quiet."

"So you agree to be my girlfriend?" I grinned.

Yeah, I said we'd wait until after our first date to try and label it, but I couldn't help teasing her. Her intentions were subtle and sweet. It was nice to bask in the glory of a budding relationship.

"Savannah, cal-"

We pulled into the driveway of the house and Maia choked on her sentence mid-way through. The quiet was bad enough, but her expression really took the cake. Her face could only be described as horror stricken as she surveyed the outside of the house. The shudders, the door, and especially the tree. If I hadn't been so consistent about burnt offerings and spirit bottles, I would've thought she saw a ghost.

"Maia, are you ok?" Ermias gasped when he spotted her in the rearview mirror.

Her face was all kinds of scrunched up, almost like she was smelling hot shit for the first time.

"Is this your house?" she gulped, unbuckling her seatbelt.

"Yeah," I nodded, pointing to the porch. "We've been here for a couple of years now."

"Only a couple of years? That tree is huge," she grimaced.

Erm was throwing the truck in park to grab our doors, but Maia slid out of her seat and into the driveway before he could even turn off the ignition. She slowly walked out to the gate

and stood in front of the tree, the furthest branch just a few inches away from her nose. She shuddered when it swayed.
"Erm had the tree for years. He just kept it in pots until we put roots down," I explained before Maia clutched her chest and began to cry.
"Are you ok? What's going on?"

Both me and Ermias were incredibly concerned. We'd transformed from happy and relaxed to terrified in an instant, and the only thing that happened was us arriving home. Maia looked tortured and terrorized, and when she first opened her mouth to speak the only sound that came out was a strangled cry.

"I have a confession," she blubbered.
"Ok," I said, my hands and feet feeling oddly tingly.
I didn't know if Ermias could feel it too, but magic was in the air.
"What's up?"
"Last month I was nearby visiting with my Granny, and I stole a peach off this branch," she admitted, pointing to the afflicted spot.
It was the same branch I had complained to Erm about, the one with the little peach that refused to grow. I tried to hex the then unknown thief but the hex backfired, and then I started to have strange dreams filled with pleading and sobbing. Familiar sobbing.

"Oh my goodness!" I shrieked while pointing my finger to the same spot. "Maia, that was you?"
"Yessss," she whined. "I thought I was cursed so I tried to pay you back with a few dollars in the mailbox but it wasn't working. And then the dreams started."
"I told you I didn't leave that $20 in the mail," Erm interjected.
"Hush," I chided while bringing my fingers to the bridge of my nose. "Wait, was that also your creepy ass truck!?"
"Why it gotta be allat?" Maia tutted.
"First off, you drive a blacked out Tacoma with storm lights. Second, $20 was overboard. It was one peach. And thirdly, I did curse you. So my bad about that."

"And this is why we don't hex people over fruit," Erm sighed. "Maia, please come here. Luci didn't mean to, she was just being a brat."
"Am I still cursed?" Maia asked from her new spot at the end of the drive. She was clearly apprehensive and probably a little freaked out, but she still inched closer. Seeing her soft face all creased with worry did something horrible to my stomach. I had never reversed-cursed before, but I'd do whatever it took to make sure Maia was good. Even giving up my grudge about

the peach.
"I don't think so but I'll lift it if you are," I offered while extending my arms to receive her.

She came quietly outside of her intermittent sniffling, her cheeks still streaked with tears.
"Was the peach at least good, Mai?"
"It-it was the best," she nodded. "I hate that I ever ate it."
I knew that feeling well. Especially after all the eating I did last night. I squeezed her tighter, accidentally causing her bosom to push up against my lil speedbumps and in that moment I was glad mind readers weren't real.
At least I thought so until I heard a screen door fly open.

"Morning!" Miss Claudette called from out her front door. "I see you've gotten friendly with my granddaughter, Maia."
Maia jumped out of my embrace with wide eyes. Her grimace thoroughly explained how we all felt with the older woman smiling at us and quirking her gray brows in lew of an expected explanation. We were busted.
"Good morning, Miss Claudette," Ermias called back. "Maia was just speaking."

Maia turned to Ermias with a subtle headshake, as if to say, *"don't lie."* Personally, I'd lie all day, everyday if my Granny caught me the morning after, but I quickly learned why that was a bad idea when it came to Miss Claudette.
"Lucianna, ain't that the same skirt and top you had on last night?" she queried while bringing her coffee to her pursed lips. "I think it is, although now it's got a hell of a whole lot of wrinkles."
"Granny, I can explain," Maia rushed.
"Nuhuh, I'm good on that explanation," Miss Claudette tutted. "I knew the plants were a warning. Just come see me when you get done being grown."
Then she disappeared back into her house in a fit of mischievous giggles.

"Now we definitely go together," Ermias whispered.
"Erm!" I chided.
"What!? Did you see how Miss Claudette was looking at us? I ain't gone have her thinking I got dishonorable intentions with her only granddaughter."
"How do you know I'm her only granddaughter?" Maia gasped.
"Sometimes we catch up over lunch," he shrugged. "We have the same birthday and Miss Claudette knows her Bourbon."

Maia went quiet again. At least this time she didn't look scared shitless. Instead she looked somber and contemplative as she focused on bits and pieces of the world around her. Leaves whipped past us, tugging our hair in different directions while our bodies crept closer. Magic was in the air again, yet unlike before, the thrilling sensation of it raced down my spine and lingered on my lips.

A kiss of destiny.

"Do you ever feel like this was meant to be?" Maia finally asked as she reached for my hand.

"Yeah," I nodded. "I was just thinking that actually."

"I knew it was weeks ago," Erm laughed. "It's nice of you two to catch up."

"Whatever," I scoffed before Maia added. "Unlock the door so we can soak and get our tea."

"I'm already getting tired of you two bossing me around," he fake huffed while doing exactly what we asked.

"Well, get used to it," we said in unison.

All three of us exchanged a look of pure joy before we broke out in laughter. Laughter that rang out so loud and strong that it shook the last glistening peach from the tree.

Epilogue

Epilogue- 18 Months Later

Maia

"Luci, I think it's breakfast time," I whispered while pecking my girlfriend's forehead.

Butter and citrus tickled my nose as Luci snuggled in closer to rub her cheek against mine. I had every intention of getting up and going to the table, but Luci's shifting caused the exposed tips of our nipples to rub. I could've recovered if it was just once, but then she did it again. Plus one more time after that for good measure. It was only eight in the morning and she was already being a problem.

"Lucianna, stop it," I groaned. "You're gonna make me wet and Erm's gonna fuss because we're gonna be late."

"Erm's always fussing," she grumbled back. "All we need is just five minutes, Mai. He doesn't even know we're up yet."

I knew the latter was likely a lie. Ermias had ears like a hawk, but lie aside, I was powerless to deny her. Especially when her soft thigh parted my own before she mounted me. She rubbed her hand in it before parting both of our lips and pressing her hot bud to mine.

"I hate how fine you are," I hissed as our hips bucked in sync.

"You love it," Luci retorted while bringing her mouth to my tight nipple. "I know you do. Look at you."

And look what I did.

It was a sight to behold, watching our squishy bodies ripple with pleasure. Watching our two fat cats slide and glide against one another with our hard, needy clits rubbing together. Ermias was going to pitch a fit if he caught us but I didn't feel the slightest drop of remorse. Instead all I felt was an impending orgasming. Nothing felt better than being ass to ass and pussy to pussy with the woman you loved.

Not even being on time.

"Do you think we have time for the cob?" Luci whined as her orgasm took her.

I pinched the stiff points of her nipples to send her over the edge, and then brought my hand to smack that fat, dimpled ass as she shook her nut out. Her relieved moan went into my ears and raced down my spine. That moan was morphine to my system and I briefly forgot that Erm and Granny would cuss us out if we were super late. I almost nodded yes before I snapped to my senses. I hated having to be the logical one, especially when her pussy was so good.

I'd buy her a Martian unicorn if she asked for it right then.

"Luci baby, you know we don't have time for the cob," I groaned.

Erm had been busy with the swing of summer and we were both craving penetration, but the cob was a bad idea. Luci was leaking all over my belly and my legs. I myself was a sticky, creamy mess. We needed food, hot showers, and a change of sheets. All of that meant we were for sure going to be late.

But I didn't wanna be double-strap-late.

"Y'all definitely don't have time for the cob," Ermias interjected.

He was already dressed for the morning when he leaned against the doorway, and while he usually wore workingmen's denim, this time he was wearing sweatpants. Heather grey ones with flecks of black and a white drawstring that strained against his waist under the weight of his hard dick. It was impressive that his voice was even despite the tent his pants were pitching. I was hoping for a much more belligerent reaction.

"You should jack it," me and Luci pleaded in unison.

We had long accepted that our relationship and initial meeting was nothing short of divine intervention, and ever since then our jinxing had gotten worse. It happened at least twice a day. Sometimes more if we were terrorizing Ermias.

"Finish cumming and go clean up," he said sternly. "We leave in one hour."

"Let us suck it a little bit, Big Daddy," Luci pouted. "You'll be less stressed."

I stuck out my tongue and flicked it in Erm's reaction, hoping to entice him into the sinner's circle. He grinned, showing off all 32 of his pearly whites, took three big steps forward, and then reached into his pants for...

A damn spray bottle.

He sprayed us with cold water like a pair misbehaving cats.

"Erm, what the fuck?" we hissed.

"You two hornballs tried to trick me, that's the fuck," he tutted. "Miss Claudette just called and asked if y'all were up. I promised her we'd be on time. I can train your throats later." That shut us up and we scrambled out of bed and raced to the bathroom. Two showers, a quick breakfast, and a coffee stop later, we were on time and headed East to our new build.

It was true that queer relationships moved at lightning speed, but that's because the gays knew what they wanted. It only took one kiss for me to know that I wanted to sleep and wake with Luci in my arms for as long as she would have me. A year later and nothing had changed so we decided to embrace the U-haul stereotypes. Now we were set to move into our dream home together in just eight months. We hadn't decided on paint colors but I had already picked out our old-lady rocking chairs and our coordinating bathrobes. So all I had to worry about right then was figuring out how to either relocate or graft the peach tree for Erm.

"How much do you think they got done?" Luci asked excitedly.
I finished reading over the inspection report with a neutral expression, trying not to give it all away.
"A good amount," I nodded.
"That means they damn near finished, Lucianna," Granny chuckled while sipping her coffee.
"Granny!" Me and Ermias chided.

Erm and I had our own sync when it came to that nosey old lady. She was forever busting our bubble, since the very first night. Which is why it was crazy that we thought it was a good idea for us to all move in together. I'd probably never know peace again, and poor Ermias? My Carebear was done for. Two women jumping on your nerves everyday was one thing, but three?
He'd be deemed a sorcerer for surviving us during the Puritan era.

"Alright everybody, take a look," Erm announced.
"It's," Luci started.
"A pile of sticks," Granny finished with a snicker.
Ok, so the house was still mostly studs, but the rooms were measured out and we now had a front door. The interior steps and drywall were being hung within the following week. We were closer to our dream home than ever before.
"Yeah, but it's *our* pile of sticks," Luci exclaimed. "Come on, Granny. Let's go check on your cottage."

They scurried off to go look at the nearly completed "cottage" before Erm could open any doors, earning them both dirty looks. It wounded Erm's pride, but they couldn't help it. The excitement was genuine. Granny had gotten on Pinterest and put together mood boards to really lean into her cottagecore living era. In reality she was actually moving into a fully functional tiny home with everything she would need to continue living independently while her helper remained within arm's reach. But Ermias was going to load the perimeter down with native plants.

That left me and Erm to tour the rest of the build. The living room, dining room, greenhouse, and guest quarters were already partitioned and loaded with everything the team would need to hang the walls. The kitchen already had flooring, and while the downstairs bathrooms were just rough drains and insulation, I had no problem envisioning how peaceful they'd be in a years' time. I could already hear the laughter of our family and friends. I could also smell the brown butter cookies, and feel the warmth of the fireplace next winter. Yeah it was mostly sticks now, but Luci was right. It was our pile of sticks.

"How you feeling, baby?" Ermias asked as he joined my side.
"Excited," I sighed. "We're on track to move in by January."
"Yeah, we don't have long left at all. I'm in disbelief. It still feels like a dream," he admitted while palming a nearby support beam.
"Everyday I have with y'all feels like a dream," I whispered while leaning against his chest.

His hand left the post and came to the small of my back to press me closer. It had been over a year and I still felt sparks when he touched me. Luci said the magic would probably never leave us. Like always, she was right. I could've stood there with him all day if we didn't have sales to hit up.
"Aight, come on," I sighed, "Let's go get them before all the good stuff gets bought up."

As soon as I finished my sentence, my phone pinged. I thought it might be Luci using her gifts, but instead it was another one of my favorite ladies. An onslaught of messages poured in before I could finish reading the first one. There were so many incoming messages that I had to silence my phone to avoid the worrying looks Erm was shooting me. Still I remained frozen in place. Watching, reading. Buzz after buzz, my eyes grew wider.
"Babe, is everything ok?" Luci asked.
I snapped out of my trance at the sound of Luci's concern and quickly gave her a reassuring smile.
"Everything's fine, baby," I nodded. "The girls are just planning our next Group Trip. This year's theme is garden party."

The end

Luci's Hung Up Tea Recipe

Makes up to twelve- 8oz cups

Dehydrated, swollen, and suffering the consequences of last night's actions? Try this herbal tea blend, designed to reduce inflammation, right your gut, and get you back on track.

For this recipe you will need:

1 clean and sanitized glass jar with a lid, capable of holding at least a cup. (An old sauce jar works fine.)

2 dried orange peels.

5 sprigs of Anise Hyssop.

6 Calendula flowers, stem removed.

1 head of Broadleaf Plantain, leaves and stems intact.

3ozs or roughly 4 large sprigs of Lemon Balm.

1 sprig of Rosemary.

¼ cup of rice or 2 silica/dry packets.

1 tbsp of Honey.

Start by giving all your herbs a good wash, then pat them completely dry. Set an oven or a clean air fryer to 150° Fahrenheit, place your herbs and orange peel on a baking tray/piece of baking paper, and roast until they are crispy and able to crumble between your fingers. For the next step, you can use a grinder, a blender or your hands. However, the herbs must be broken apart until the herbs appear homogeneous and uniform in size. Once grinding is complete, place your rice or dry packs in the bottom of your clean jar, add your tea, and seal your jar. To brew, bring 1 cup of water to a boil, add 1 teaspoon of your tea mixture to a tea ball, strainer, or loose leaf tea bag, and place in your favorite mug along with a tablespoon of honey. Pour your water over your tea, and let seep uncovered for 5-7 minutes. Tea should be a clouded golden color. Drink warm alongside a cookie, a plate of pancakes, or a piece of toast with extra butter. **Pregnant persons should use caution, drinking Rosemary tea may induce premature labor.**

Ermias' Herb Breakfast Potatoes

Serves two-four Est time: 1hr

C raving carbs after a late night or an early morning? Gather up all your greenery and make these savory, crispy potatoes guaranteed to take any morning from a zero to an hero.

For this recipe you'll need:

1. One pound of golden Yukon potatoes

2. 3 cloves of garlic

3. 1 medium shallot

4. 3 sprigs of fresh rosemary or 1tbsp dried

5. 2 sprigs fresh tarragon or 1tsp dried

6. 2 sprigs fresh thyme or 1tsp dried

7. 1 tsp nutmeg

8. 1tbsp black pepper

9. 1½ tsp salt

10. 1 tsp onion powder

11. 1 tsp garlic powder

12. 1 tbsp olive or canola oil

13. 1 tsp of cornstarch

Preheat your oven to 400 Fahrenheit while you bring 4 cups of water to a boil. Wash, dry, and then cube your potatoes into medium pieces, keeping them uniform to ensure even cooking. Place cubed potatoes in the boiling water and allow them to cook 15-20 minutes until partially softened. While your potatoes are going through the initial cook, prepare your shallots and garlic by chopping them finely and setting them aside. Once potatoes reach medium firmness, drain the water and allow them to cool for ten minutes. After the potatoes are cool add them along with your seasonings, herbs, cornstarch, and oil into a large bowl, and toss everything until it's fully coated. Transfer the seasoned potatoes onto a cast iron skillet or a lined baking sheet, and bake for 25-30 minutes or until golden brown and fragrant. Serve along side some jammy-yolked eggs, thick sliced bacon, and wheat toast. Or double your batch and bring them to your auntie's house to redeem that batch of potato salad you made last Thanksgiving. You know the one. If you make this recipe, please tag me! Enjoy!

Thank You!

Hey Friendddd! So obviously, you finished the book, and I just wanted to take a moment to say thank you. I recently passed my two year publishing anniversary and wow, what a way we have come. From conquering big wide knowledge gaps, to building ARC teams, and even my first signing event, y'all have held me down. Thank you so so much for all the love and support. I really could not ask for a better literary community, and as always, I look forward to catching you at the next book!

P.S.

If you liked this book, please consider leaving me a review. It helps others in the community discover my work!

About the author

A ria is a die-hard romantic and her main goal is to always be drying her eyes from something sickly sweet. She has been dreaming up romance stories since she was seven years old, with the first one being a Toy Story fanfic. She's also a Neo-soul and R&B enthusiast who's forever got a song stuck in her head. You can find her looking for good food, reading, writing, or enjoying time with her family in her free time. She lives happily in Saint Louis, Missouri with her middle school sweetheart-turned-husband and their adorably chaotic son. Her dream is to one day write inclusive stories that center BIPOC full-time, but for now, she labors in fraud as a working stay-at-home mom.

Also by Aria Daze

Glory

"**I** wanted everything all the time. Boys, girls, fae, theys, and thems. I wanted to eat braised short ribs and red-skin mashed potatoes while sipping an elaborate drink that contained no alcohol. I wanted to be enshrined in a candle too pretty to burn and memorialized in affectionate poetry detailing my midnight skin. I wanted to hold Cash and be held by Frankie. I wanted them both. Both."

Gloria Esther King is living up to what it means to be a preacher's daughter: Wild, sneaky, and promiscuous. She had no plans to give up the single life, but the twenty-seven-year-old re-evalutaes her life choices, finding herself stuck between heaven and hell after a routine night out goes wrong.

One For The Team

Despite what her recent ex-boyfriend thinks, Chrissy Hawkins has options.

As the beloved mascot for the Minnesota Hares, she's surrounded by beautiful men every week. But none more so than Blessing Harrel. The high-energy hockey center has had his eye on her since she joined the team even though she remained needlessly loyal to her so-called boyfriend. However, he isn't the only one pursuing Chrissy, and it's an unfair fight where Emery Greene and Thaxton Paul are concerned. All three of them are shooting their shot both on and off the ice. So what will happen when neither of them can take a back seat on their feelings for Chrissy? Will she choose? Or will she take one for the team?

Burry The Hatchette

"Andrea Hatchette, a woman after my own soulless void of a heart. Will you do me the honor of being my wife?"

Lots of women dream of moments like this. A calm evening. A party on the lake surrounded by her family and friends. A handsome, rich, educated man asking for their hand in marriage in the middle of a fancy-ass yacht with a big-ass ring. Except for Andrea. Marrying her lifelong enemy, Nathaniel Burry, is her worst nightmare. Still, she knows she has no other choice if she doesn't want to be disowned and thrown from the company she helped build. She supposes there could be worse fates than marrying a billionaire. Right?

Meanwhile, Nat has a plan. Being forced to take a wife isn't the picture of peace he had five years previous, but he's willing to make the best of it with Andrea. After all, even villains deserve happy endings. Can these two find middle ground and make it work, or will they drown in a storm of their own creation?